John Strange Winter

Army Society

Life in a Garrison Town - A Discursive Story. Seventh Edition

John Strange Winter

Army Society
Life in a Garrison Town - A Discursive Story. Seventh Edition

ISBN/EAN: 9783337058814

Printed in Europe, USA, Canada, Australia, Japan

Cover: Foto ©Andreas Hilbeck / pixelio.de

More available books at **www.hansebooks.com**

PUBLIC OPINION

the only Weekly Journal which contains the opinions of e Press throughout the World on all the great Political d Social Topics of the Day—Home and Foreign—thereby ving the most varied and accurate information on all subjects of interest.

EVERY FRIDAY, PRICE 2d.

tablished 25 Years. Annual Subscription, 10s. 10d., post free.

ffice: 11, SOUTHAMPTON ST., STRAND,

ARMY SOCIETY:

LIFE IN A GARRISON TOWN.

A Discursive Story.

BY

JOHN STRANGE WINTER,

AUTHOR OF

"CAVALRY LIFE," "BOOTLES' BABY," "HOUP-LA," "ON MARCH,"
"IN QUARTERS," "PLUCK!" "REGIMENTAL LEGENDS,"
ETC.

"What is life, Father?"
"A battle, my child!
Where the strongest lance may fall,
And the wariest eyes may be beguiled,
And the stoutest heart may quail;
Where the foes are gathered on ev'ry hand,
And rest not day or night,
And the feeble little ones must stand
In the thickest of the fight."
Heaven and Earth.

Seventh Edition.

LONDON: F. V. WHITE & CO.,
31 SOUTHAMPTON STREET, STRAND, W.C.

1887.

Dedication.

TO MY ONLY BROTHER,

To whose sympathetic and ever-ready encouragement during many years of literary effort, I owe
more than I can ever estimate, I affectionately
dedicate these pages.

JOHN STRANGE WINTER.

Putney, *May* 1886.

CONTENTS.

ARMY SOCIETY.

SIDELIGHT.

IN A GARRISON TOWN.

QUESTION:—What elements constitute Army Society?

ANSWER:—Three; mothers, daughters, and the Army.

ARMY SOCIETY.

CHAPTER I.

ON A FALSE SCENT.

IT was well known to everybody in the good old city of Blankhampton that Polly Antrobus might, if she had played her cards a shade better, have married the Honourable Eliot Cardella, a popular and exceedingly handsome cavalry officer, and the younger son of the rich and noble Earl of Mallinbro'.

Not unreasonably, people thought and said it would have been a splendid match for the daughter of a country attorney, whose practice was not of the best as far as the social position of his clients went, and who was known to do a good deal in the money-lending line, and on the sixty per cent. principle.

But alack, alas, for the tide which must be
taken at the flood! Polly, and moreover Polly's
papa and mamma, wished for a higher, stronger,
fuller tide than served just then in the person of
the Honourable Eliot Cardella—they wished for
what was, in fact, quite a matrimonial spring-
tide; and in waiting for it Polly missed both.

It was no new story—only a new reading of
that old, old tale of the dog who dropped the
substance for the shadow. For Polly and her
people, who had at first found Eliot Cardella
everything that was desirable, changed their
opinion entirely when his only brother, Lord
Cardella, appeared upon the scene and at once
began to make the most outrageous love to his
brother's *fiancée:* all Blankhampton knew that
he had done it in order to gain his brother's
freedom.

Now Eliot, who had been very neatly trapped
into the engagement, would have stuck to Polly
through thick and thin, even if by doing so he
would have ruined his whole life, had Polly
stuck to him. But Polly did not do so: on
the contrary, dazzled by the glitter of a title
which was not by courtesy, and pining for the
coronet of a countess with which to bind her
fair brows, and for the famous Mallinbro' diamonds to shine and twinkle about her white
throat, Polly sent him about his business with
promptitude and decision; whereupon Lord Cardella took himself off about *his* business also,

leaving the fair Polly to dree her weird over a card marked P.P.C., having also the pleasant consciousness that everybody in the town was laughing at her, and that most people were thoroughly enjoying her discomfiture.

Mrs Hugh Antrobus, her mother—"Mrs Hugh" everyone called her—was eloquent on the subject. "The fa-ct *is*," she said confidentially to Mr Antrobus and Polly, "the fa-ct *is*, we have made a great mistake in knowing the Cuirassiers on an *im*-proper footing."

"I quite agree with you there, Mariana," said Hugh Antrobus decidedly.

Now, as a matter of fact, they had never known the Cuirassiers (as a regiment) on any footing, except that Hugh Antrobus had called on the mess, receiving in return two cards left by two gentlemen who did not even ask whether he happened to be at home or not; further, they had scraped acquaintance with the Paymaster, whose back windows overlooked the garden of the River House, and through him they contrived almost to hook the Honourable Eliot Cardella.

"Now," Mrs Hugh went on, with a certain lingering over her words which was a characteristic of hers; "I have qui-te made up my mind about one thing, and that *is*, that with the new regiment we must take a different stand. It ne-vah does to know *tho-se* sort of people —it nev-ah pays, and between you and I"

— she invariably used the nominative — " we must for the future take a *to*-tally different stand."

" Oh ! no, no ; you're quite right, Mariana, it never pays," agreed her lord and master, with an uncomfortable remembrance of the cards left by the Cuirassiers, and a reminder to himself that they had not then known *those* kind of people.

" Therefore I shall call upon the Colonel's wife *im*-mediately," his wife went on briskly. " It will be better in ev-ery respect ; it puts one on such a different footing with the reg-iment. And we must *en*-tertain them *di*-rectly. It is *no* use, Hugh, waiting to *get* to know people ; *we* must take the initiative."

So "*we*" did take the initiative, and Mrs Hugh and Polly called on the Colonel's wife before that lady had been in Blankhampton a week ; and to Mrs Hugh's triumph and delight, Mrs Trelawney greeted them with effusion, welcomed them, so to speak, with open arms.

Mrs Hugh looked significantly at Polly as much as to say — " See what I have accomplished !" while Polly looked pretty and said nothing.

" Is Blankhampton a pleasant place ? " Mrs Trelawney asked.

" Well, so-so," Mrs Hugh replied ; " ve-ry poor ; ve-ry proud ; ve-ry *ex*-clusive."

One or two officers of the Yellow Horse had

spoken of it to their chief's wife as a first-rate hunting centre, and Mrs Trelawney mentioned it.

"Yes, that is so," Mrs Hugh answered; "and there are some good balls; but, as a rule, it is ra-ther a dull place. Yes, there are good ball-rooms, and good balls too. Two county-balls—the Hunt—the Off-icers'," with a little laugh, "and the Yeo-manry; a *very* good ball that, but the invitations are dreadfully difficult to obtain;" and then she added carelessly,—"We have ours from the ABBOT-ABBOTS of ABBOTSWELL."

"Oh! really; good people the Abbots," observed Mrs Trelawney, greatly amused by her visitor's Roman capital style of mentioning the family.

"Oh! ve-ry good family," Mrs Hugh replied.

She quite, however, omitted to mention that Hugh Antrobus had once, some years back, hidden under his roof for a week or more a young scion of the house of Abbot, who was what is vulgarly called "wanted" by the police, contriving then to get him "shipped off foreign" in the guise or disguise, which you will, of a countryman, for which good service the head of the house wrote the name of Antrobus upon his game-list, and promised moreover to do him any favour he might ask, never dreaming that the very first request would be for invitations to the Yeomanry ball, where the company of second-rate attorneys is not usually desired or to be found.

However, though Mrs Hugh had not forgotten the trifling circumstance, it is not always expedient to tell all one knows : for the matter of that, it was quite as well that Mrs Hugh was not in the habit of following that practice, for her disclosures would indeed have been startling.

After some more conversation, during which Mrs Hugh learned that Mrs Trelawney's youngest child had been born in the Suez Canal on the way home from India, and named Julia Serapis in consequence, a little divertissement came in the shape of a tall dragoon wearing evening clothes and bearing a tea-tray.

Yes, Mrs Hugh would take a cup, and over it she waxed more friendly and confidential than ever.

"You have a good many off-icers in your regiment ? " she remarked, in a questioning tone.

Mrs Trelawney stared in amazement at this. " Yes, the usual strength," she answered.

" Ah ! yes. And are there many *married* people ? "

" Not many. No ! only ourselves and the senior captain, whose wife is not likely to be here at all this summer. She met with a serious accident last year at Simla ; her carriage was upset over a chud, and she was frightfully hurt. I fancy she will remain with her own people for the present. But the two doctors are married; the assistant surgeon's wife is little more than a bride, and very rich: a charming girl too she is."

" Really ! I intend calling upon her to-morrow. They are staying just opposite to us;" but in truth Mrs Hugh had intended doing nothing of the kind, having classed Mrs Marsden in her own mind as being amongst *those* sort of people.

" And have you any *weal*-thy men amongst the off-icers ? " she asked carelessly.

" Oh, ho ! " thought the Colonel's wife ; " wants a rich husband for the pretty daughter. What a joke !"

" Only two really eligible men," she made haste to reply, " both very young—mere boys."

" Oh, indeed ! And their names ? " in a tone of supreme indifference, as if she was only pursuing the subject in order to make conversation.

" One is called Devreux, the other Heywood—enormously rich both of them, and such pleasant boys," Mrs Trelawney answered.

At this point another divertissement came in the shape of a visitor, a divertissement regarded by Mrs Hugh in the light of a tiresome interruption, until she heard the name of the visitor announced by the big dragoon.

"Lord Alfred Pierrepoint!"

Lord Alfred walked across the room and shook hands with the lady of the house, found himself a chair, and remarked that it was a fearfully cold day.

Mrs Trelawney asked if he would have a cup of tea.

"Oh! tha-anks," he answered, with a look at Mrs Hugh.

Then he laid his hat, stick, and gloves on the little table at his elbow; and, as he took the cup, said, "Tha-anks" again, with a look at Polly, which he did not repeat.

Lord Alfred was clumsy and loutish-looking, yet Mrs Hugh expanded with pride till she very nearly overflowed her chair—for Lord Alfred Pierrepoint was, she very well knew, the son of a marquis, one of the noblest families in the three kingdoms. She rose presently to take leave, feeling positively dizzy with the magnitude of her success; she beamed "with a smile that was childlike and bland" upon Lord Alfred when he stood up as she shook both Mrs Trelawney's hands, and went away, passing through the streets with quite an indulgent air to all she met— the indulgent air of a victor returning from the scene of her triumphs. Indeed, all the little hanging jet ornaments upon her bonnet seemed to jingle and tinkle a triumphal march in miniature.

And if only Polly could manage to secure Lord Alfred — what a triumph that would be. Mrs Hugh gave her head an extra wave at the mere possibility of such a thing, and set all the little ornaments tinkling again in what was positively a millinery symphony.

How it would let those unprincipled, odious, utterly detestable Cardellas see! *How* it would pay off dozens of old scores among Blankhampton folk—hints, smiles, looks, and. worst of all, open condolences. Already in imagination Mrs Hugh regarded Polly as, "my daughter, Lady Alfred Pierrepoint."

SIDELIGHT.

MRS HUGH ANTROBUS.

"I REALLY don't think that I care very much about Sundays," said Mrs Hugh Antrobus to her friend Mrs Dallas, as they walked home from church together one lovely summer morning: she had spent a very profitable hour and a half in church,—not in religious meditations, but deep in a calculation as to whether she could get the servants to do without meat for supper, and whether the two younger girls could make their frocks last a little longer. "Sunday interferes so with all one's regular routine," she went on blandly: "and it's such a tiresome day — like a day wasted!"

"Oh! dear, Mrs Hugh!" cried Mrs Dallas, "you would not surely do away with the day of rest?"

"The day of hindrance," cried Mrs Hugh, with her oiliest laugh, "hindrance to all my plans. Oh! dear, yes, I could dispense with Sunday very well. Polly—did you put a shilling in the bag?"

"Yes, mamma," said Polly promptly.

"That's right. Well, Mrs Dallas," to her friend; "you'll come in after church this evening and have supper with us, won't you? Dear mamma is here — she came yesterday."

"Oh! I don't know if Mr Dallas—"

"Oh! yes, de-ah, do come. Hugh likes to sing a few hymns on Sunday evening, and the children enjoy it. You will come, won't you, de-ah?"

"I'll see what Mr Dallas says?"

"Very well; but remember I shall count upon you," was Mrs Hugh's airy rejoinder.

CHAPTER II.

BUT that very fertile imagination of Mrs Hugh's had led her altogether to reckon without her host. So far as Polly was concerned, Lord Alfred was impractible, as she would have realised instantly could she have stayed unseen in Mrs Trelawney's drawing-room, after the door had closed behind herself and Polly. She would have seen Lord Alfred standing on the hearth, his society manner and his "tha-anks" quite gone, and in their stead an air of being very much at home indeed; in fact, he took hold of Mrs Trelawney's arm and drew her very near to him.

"How's your cold to-day, Rosey?" he asked tenderly: Mrs Hugh would have realised instantly, had she heard it, that all the love this noble lord had to give (at present) was given to the not very handsome, and no longer very young, wife of his commanding officer.

"Very bad, Taff, very bad; I feel as stupid as an owl," she answered.

"I don't at all wonder. Who was that old frump?"

"A Mrs Antrobus. I don't know anything more about her."

"H—m! Prodigious old party."

"Yes—perhaps. But the girl is lovely," in a tone she tried hard to make hearty.

"Lovely? Didn't see it myself—all red and white like a dairy-maid, with a slobbery mouth. Not my style at all," said Lord Alfred, with uncompromising plainness. "Didn't strike me as very good form either. What are they? Who's the father when he's at home?"

"I haven't a notion. Mrs Antrobus was just beginning to pump me as to the eligible men in the regiment, when you came in and put a stop to it. I—it was too bad of me—" with a laugh full of mischief—"but I told her there were only two really rich ones."

"Yes?" questioningly. "Which two?"

"Devreux and Heywood."

Lord Alfred postively roared.

"Upon my soul, Rosey, you are the very cleverest woman I ever had the good fortune to come across,—just my usual ill-luck that the Colonel met you before I did. I wonder what those fellows will say?"

" You'll tell them ? "

" I should think so. They'll be asked to
dinner forthwith without doubt."

" You too," with the least little ring of
jealousy in her voice.

" Oh! I daresay. I sha'n't go though; I
should never be rid of them again. That's the
worst of having a handle to one's name. There
is no chance of being overlooked, or mistaken
for anybody else. It's a great nuisance, and
really I don't know that it has any advantages
on the other hand."

Alas for Mrs Hugh's visions—fairy visions of
" my daughter, Lady Alfred Pierrepoint ! "

Yet, after all, Lord Alfred did once dine at
the River House, because the Trelawneys were
asked, and he usually went wherever Mrs
Trelawney did.

It must be confessed that, on the whole, that
party was a dismal failure. Lord Alfred, finding himself separated from Mrs Trelawney by
the whole length of the dinner-table, turned
sulky, and paid attention to nothing but the
wine, which he afterwards pronounced execrable.
Then, as soon as he entered the drawing-room,
he made for a vacant place at Mrs Trelawney's
side, and there he remained a fixture, declining
on any pretext whatever to be dislodged until
the party broke up.

It is true they asked him again, more than
once, but as he could sit on the same sofa with

Mrs Trelawney every day of his life, he did not see enduring two hours of misery that he might do so in the River House drawing-room.

However, the intimacy between the Colonel's wife and the family at the River House progressed amazingly ; and the delight of it never seemed to pall upon Mrs Hugh's soul. In fact, the whole family of the Antrobuses paraded their friendship in high quarters in every manner imaginable. Thus at the Winter Garden, when the band of the Yellow Horse was playing, might be heard,—

"To-to! To-to! where's pap-ah?"

"Oh! pap-ah's with the COLONEL!"

Or in this fashion,—

"Baby! baby! where's your mother?"

"I don't know, papa. She's somewhere with Mrs Trelaw-ney!"

Or after this manner,—

"Baby! baby! where is To-to?"

"Oh! To-to and Polly have gone to see the fairy fountain with the COLONEL."

And so on.

Indeed, it became a matter of considerable amusement to some people, more accustomed to that class of society than the Antrobuses, to see how often the COLONEL and Mrs Trelaw-ney could be brought into their conversations.

"Such a joke the other day," said sharp Miss To-to. "The COLONEL and Mrs Trelaw-ney were dining with us, and the COLONEL said,—

'Oh! by the way, Rosey wants to have a stall
at the Parish' (they always call Blankhampton
Cathedral "the Parish"), 'how am I to get
one for her?' 'Why don't you call on the
Dean?' said I. 'Call on the Dean,' he repeated
—and he said it in such a doubtful kind of
way—'Oh! but there are a lot of Miss Deans,
aren't there?' 'Only three,' I told him. 'Oh!'
said the COLONEL, in such a comical tone, 'but
it's a formidable matter facing three Miss
Deans.'"

Now some few of the many people who
heard this story, who were able to read between
the lines, thought it a trifle odd that a married
Colonel of good family should be afraid of the
Dean's daughters; but they naturally kept
their thoughts to themselves, at least as far
as the Antrobuses were concerned, so the farce
was played on and progressed.

"Strictly between you and I," said Mrs Hugh
one day to a friend, "Polly has a cold manner.
I believe Mr Devreux admired her *im*-mensely
—indeed, how could he help it? But Polly has
not encouraged him. Not that it matters, however, for he has already had some conversation
with Hugh, and though we don't speak of it to
every one, there is no harm in my telling you
that he has *ul*-terior views respecting To-to."

"How old is To-to?" the lady asked, thinking of that young lady's skinny shanks and
unformed childish person.

' Not yet sixteen—much too young to dre-am
of anything of that kind at present. Oh! they
are *quite ul*-terior views—*quite* in the future."

Well, to the intense delight or such of the
good people of Blankhampton as happened to
be in the secret, this pretty play was played
on all through the early half of the winter,
that is, until the season of Christmas was over,
and the New Year's gaieties came on, and the
invitations for the far-famed Yeomanry ball
were sent out.

During all that time the Antrobus' old
friends found them almost unapproachable, on
account of the all-engrossing intimacy with
the Colonel of the Yellow Horse and Mrs Trelaw-ney, while on the few occasions when they
condescended to remember older but less distinguished friends, they literally flaunted the
new ones in their faces.

" Mr Antrobus was dining with the COLONEL,"
Mrs Hugh might be heard to say at such times,
in her most oily tones, and with a superior smile
upon her fat face. "At MESS, you know, and he
heard so-and-so—"

Or, "Mrs Trelaw-ney was asking me the
other day if I could recommend a really *good*
HEAD-nurse for her baby."

And at all times she was ready and willing to
descant on the beauties and excellencies of Lord
Alfred Pierrepoint's character and manner,—

" A thorough aristocrat — of COURSE," she

would say in her own peculiar italicised style.
" Ve-ry unapproachable—won't take the trouble,
in fa-ct, to lay himself out to please *cv*-ery-
body"—as if Lord Alfred had not only offered
to lay down himself but his very life for her
and hers—"yet a *very* charming man when you
come to know him *in*-timately."

Well, in due course the invitations for the
Yeomanry ball were sent out, and by dint of
the usual application to the Abbot-Abbots, the
Antrobuses obtained theirs. And then, in the
very midst of their anxious efforts that Polly
should hit upon something in dress very striking and very becoming, a piece of information
crept out in Blankhampton society, and spread
over the old city, flying very quickly towards
the River House, where it burst upon the Antrobuses as with the shock of a bomb-shell.

Mrs Trelawney had not been invited !

It was inexplicable ! It was absurd ! It was
monstrous !· So Mrs Hugh declared—and forthwith a story was got up and freely circulated
to the effect that Lord Blankhampton, the
senior captain of the Blankhampton Yeomanry,
had called personally upon the Colonel's wife,
carrying with him a card of invitation, with a
thousand apologies for the oversight which had
prevented a longer invitation.

But, for all that, no card of invitation was
ever received by the Colonel's wife, for the very
good and sufficient reason that one was never

sent to her by Lord Blankhampton or anyone else; and the real facts of the case were these.

It happened that the Earl of Mallinbro', the colonel of the Blankhampton Yeomanry, had a niece married to the Honourable Algernon Dacre, then commanding the 110th Hussars, and just at the time that the Yeomanry were beginning to think about their ball, the Dacres came home from India on a year's leave of absence, and arrived at the Castle on a visit. The very first evening, it happened that the lists for the ball were being looked over, and Colonel Dacre glanced down them.

"'Trelawney,'" said he sharply, "'and Mrs Trelawney'; have you the Yellow Horse here?"

"Yes," replied Lord Mallinbro'; "they've been here some time, but we have seen nothing of them. My lady has never called; we've been away so long. I believe she intends to call on everyone this week."

"My dear lord!" Colonel Dacre exclaimed, "Lady Mallinbro' cannot call on Mrs Trelawney. I wonder you have never heard—"

"We have heard nothing," Lord Mallinbro' interrupted. "We haven't seen a soul: we only got here yesterday."

"Then, if you make inquiries, I think you will find that Mrs Trelawney, though *she* has been here some time, has not seen a soul either."

"Oh-h! and do you know anything of her?"

"Rather! I know that her life, both before

and after her marriage, prevented her from being received even in Anglo-Indian society, which as you know is lenient, because black sheep and white are compelled to mingle in friendliness in the land which we hold by the sword, and so are drawn together despite many a fault and failing which would not be overlooked at home. Of course a general haziness as to the date of a marriage ceremony can be overlooked, but when the same haziness seems to extend over the question, 'Which is the husband?' why—"

"Oh! really; you don't say so. Who is the other man?"

"Taff Pierrepoint."

"You don't mean it!" cried Lord Mallinbro'.

"Oh! yes, I do. Mrs Trelawney's preference for Taff's society is well known all over the Punjaub."

And there the matter ended: Anglo-Indian society had declined to receive Mrs Trelawney, and "the swim" in Blankhampton and its neighbourhood had followed suit. It was no use arguing about it or gainsaying it, it was of less use to spread contradictory reports, for nobody believed them, and Mrs Hugh was only laughed at for clinging so desperately to her distinguished friends, and making a parade of what was indeed a new trait in her character, a profession of charity and a desire always to believe the best until the worst is forced upon you.

But the woman was indomitable! When she found that the new charity idea was no good, she pulled herself together, so to speak, and enlarged in a severe manner upon "these ARMY people who come and go—here to-day and gone to-morrow, nobody knowing *who* or *what* they are;" forgetting altogether what her hearers remembered only too well, the fact that had she been even but on the outer edge of "the swim," she would have known within a week exactly who and what these particular army people happened to be.

And that was the end of Mrs Hugh's first plunge into army society.

However, Mrs Hugh, in her own mind at all events, lived the mistake down, and vowed to eschew officers' wives entirely for the future, at least until she might be absolutely assured of their respectability. Therefore, in accordance with that laudable resolution, she laid her plans for attacking the regiment which in time relieved the Yellow Horse, and took up its quarters in Blankhampton Barracks.

SIDELIGHT.

POLLY ANTROBUS.

SHE was a good girl, but very foolish. Her favourite attitude was one of pretty dutifulness, and her powers of conversation were very limited. There is, however, one very brilliant utterance of hers on record, which was given to the world on an occasion when she was constrained to make conversation with a gentleman afflicted by terrible shyness. *N.B.*—The gentleman was what is called in slang phraseology "a catch."

"Do you like afternoon dances?" asked Polly.

"Oh—er—awfully," said he.

"Some people don't care about them."

"N—no—I—I believe not," in an agony of shyness.

"And what is *your* favourite pursuit?"

She was very sorry for him, and his shyness made her feel shy too.

" Oh—er—er—model-farming, I think."

Now Polly knew nothing about farming, model or otherwise, so the two came to a dead block, and stood, he looking admiringly at her, she gazing away over the glowing corn-fields to the blue hills half-a-dozen miles away, for the dance was not in Blankhampton but at a pleasant manor house some miles from that town.

" The country is looking very well," said the " catch," in a burst of confidence.

" Yes," answered Polly, looking all round the landscape. " And there's a good deal of land about here, isn't there ? "

CHAPTER III.

"A VERY PUSHING LITTLE PERSON."

IT was in the pleasant month of April that the Yellow Horse got their route and went away by detachments from the city of Blankhampton; and it was just about the same time that other important changes occurred also.

In the first place, Blankhampton became the headquarters of the centre, or district, in which it lay and in the second, a Mrs Trafford arrived in the town and established herself in a house not far from "the Parish"; one of a row known as St Eve's, and taking about the same position in Blankhampton that Carlton House Terrace does in London.

These were the two great changes, which, in the spring of 188—, came upon the city which Mrs Hugh Antrobus had described as ve-ry poor, ve-ry proud, and ve-ry *exclusive*. It was not a

bad description of the old place, or rather of its
people. Blankhampton was poor—very poor—
so poor that pretty nearly *anything* or anybody
with a little money was soon able to get almost
to the top of the social tree. And it was very
proud ; though of what, heaven above only knew.
Exclusive ; though why and wherefore, was a
puzzle to anyone who knew the genealogy of
the inhabitants.

For Blankhampton was a grandfatherless sort
of place; what Mrs Hugh, as everyone familiarly
called her, was accustomed to describe as a place
where everybody was much of a muchness ; a
remark not altogether relished or agreed with
by all her hearers; one of whom was heard to
remark sharply,—"Blankhampton people may
be pretty much alike in the matter of *grand-
fathers*, but some of us had fathers and some
of us had *not*." But that is somewhat beside
my story.

Naturally enough, everybody was in a high
state of delight when the military headquarters
arrived in the city and settled themselves in a
long block of red-brick buildings, bearing the
broad arrow of the Government here and there,
and with a fine specimen of Tommy Atkins
pacing up and down in front of the principal
entrance.

For, of course, this influx of army men and
their belongings was an uncommonly good thing
for the town ; giving the old place quite an air

of excitement whilst the shaking-down process continued. And whilst this was going on the headquarters of the 25th Dragoons (the Black Horse), marched into Blankhampton barracks, and found that the headquarters of the outgoing regiment were still in possession, but timed to march out on the following morning.

Of course there was a great fuss between the two sets of officers.

"Hullo, Urquhart; how d'do — how d'do? Haven't seen you for ages," from Trelawney.

"No, by Jove! never since we were at Sandhurst together," in reply from Urquhart "What a young rip you were in those days."

"I suppose I was: got all that knocked out of me ages since. By Jove! sir, if I were to tell you some incidents of my life since you and I last met, I should make your hair stand on end; yes, literally stand on end, by Jove!"

Urquhart linked his arm in the other's.

"Tell me about it, old boy," he said persuasively, struck by Trelawney's tone. "What have you been after?"

Colonel Trelawney half twisted himself away from his old friend's friendly grasp.

"No, it's no use raking up old sores now; *I've* got to bear 'em, and you can't help me," he answered. "And that's the hardest nut of all— it's got to be borne—to see one's wife mixing with a lot of fifth-rate cads because one was an idiot ten years ago; but there, I'd rather not

talk about it.   Tell me about yourself.   Are you
married ? "

"Married !   No, not I," with a short laugh.

"Ah! the old Tom Urquhart.   Well, I don't
know that you're not the best off.   There are
worse things in this life than being an old
bachelor.   But how is it you're not married?
What became of—"

"*Don't !*" put in Urquhart sharply, pale to
his very lips.   "I am as I am; never mind the
past; it is past, and that is enough.   Tell me
of yourself—of your wife.   Is she still in the
town ? "

"Oh, yes; she leaves on Thursday."

"Really, I wish you'd take me down to call
on her.   I should like to see her immensely."

"Would you ?" in a half doubtful tone.   "I'll
take you, of course, if you like, but Rosey's
not often at home at this hour.   Still I'm
going home now, and I'll drive you down if
you'll come straight away.   If Rosey's out,
you can see the children."

"Oh! there are children ?" with a laugh.

"Yes—three youngsters; the very light of my
eyes, Tom—the pride of my life."   From which
Colonel Urquhart drew the not unnatural con-
clusion that Mrs Trelawney was neither the one
nor the other.

As the two commanding officers drove out
of the barracks together, one of the newcomers,
who was standing in a group of men just

outside the door of the mess-rooms, turned
and watched the carriage out of sight.

"Urquhart seems to be an old friend of your
colonel's," he said to one of the Yellow Horse.

"Yes, evidently," returned the other. "Looks
an uncommonly good fellow, your chief."

"Oh, rather, yes" The speaker was Marcus
Orford, only son and heir of Lord Ceespring.
"Used to be the very best fellow in the
world. He's gone off since he had command
of the regiment; does the heavy father style
of business, and don't seem to see the fun of
anything but field-days and official returns.
Ah!" shaking his head dolefully, "it was a
bad day for the Black Horse when Urquhart
took to the heavy father style of business. I
hate to see a good man gone wrong in that
way; it's worse that when he gets married"

"I don't know; that depends on the wife,
particularly if he commands a regiment."

"Think so? What's your chief's wife like?"

"To look at? Oh, not much—pretty plain
on the whole."

"No; I didn't mean to look at. I meant in
herself," Orford returned.

The other man, whose name was Crecy,
changed the conversation by putting a question to Marcus Orford, fair and straight.

"I wish you'd walk into town with me,"
he asked. "I've got some bills to pay. Will
you?"

"Oh, yes, I shall be very glad. You can put me up to the lions," Orford answered.

So the two men followed on foot the direction which the two commanding officers had taken in Colonel Trelawney's carriage, and then Marcus Orford was able to put a question which was burning his bump of curiosity as money burns a hole in some folk's pockets.

"Why did you shut me up about your Colonel's wife?" he asked.

"Because Taff Pierrepoint was standing by," Crecy answered.

"But what has Taff Pierrepoint to do with her? Is he her brother, or what?"

"Anything but her brother," said Crecy with a laugh. "He's her — her — great admirer; that's all."

"But I thought you said she was plain."

"So she is—very," Crecy replied. "But the Colonel's very fond of her, apparently, and Taff's completely gone upon her."

"Is she young?"

"Young? Lord, no; forty odd!"

"H—m; that's funny. Hullo, who's this benignant old party?" as Crecy took off his hat in answer to a bow from a vast and smiling elderly lady.

"Oh, that Mrs Hugh Antrobus. Queer old soul; always make me think of a turtle waddling along. Has a pretty daughter,

though, awfully pretty. Don't know if I
shouldn't have gone for her under some
circumstances—that is, if I'd been as rich as
—as—a Jew."

"As well for you that you're not. What
sort of people are they?"

"Oh, very second-rate — quite the citizen
style of thing. I did hear that she was engaged once to Cardella of the Cuirassiers, but
I never believed it. It isn't common-sense
that Cardella would have looked at a girl
like that, however pretty she might be, and
in his own neighbourhood too. Why, his
father never would have stood it to begin
with."

"I believe it was true though. I remember
Eliot telling me something about it. Her
name was Polly?"

"Yes; the fair Polly we call her," answered
Crecy.

"And she's very pretty?" Orford asked.

"Oh, yes, very."

"What sort of prettiness? Anything like
'Mamma'?"

"Not at all. No; really pretty, with a
dazzlingly fair complexion — regular rose and
lily, and all that, you know."

"Ah, really;" then there was a moment's
pause, after which Orford spoke again. "Did
you know Eliot Cardella?"

"Oh, yes. What a splendid fellow he was."

" Yes. Nice chap, very. He and I were at school together. Wretched thing his dying out there as he did."

" Very. Never could tell what took him out at all. Never could see the force of going to India myself, not even for a poor man. You get a big income, of course, but then you have to spend a bigger one to live in anything like ordinary comfort. And yet fellows go out there, shoals of them, and curse and swear at the place the whole time they're in it, and fret and worry and pine to come home, when all the time they've not got a ha'pennyworth of advantage from being there. Rather the contrary, in fact, for it's ten chances to one that they get mixed up with some woman or other in a way that simply couldn't happen at home."

" Yes—other fellow's wives," laughed Orford.

" Yes, that's so; and if it happens to be somebody who isn't some other fellow's wife, why, that's all the worse for you, for ten chances to one you've got to make her yours. Oh! I never could see the force of serving in India myself."

" Nor I. By-the-bye, who was that lady who passed you just now ? "

" A Mrs Trafford. Lives in St Eve's, which is the Elysium of Blankhampton householders. She's only been here a short time."

" Who is she ? "

C

"Can't say, I'm sure. Very pushing little person. I did hear someone or other say she'd been a national schoolmistress, who married her parson. Can't say if it's true. Should say it's not at all unlikely, judging by appearances."

"And the girl ? "

"Which girl ? The little one's her daughter."

"No ; I meant the other—the tall one."

"Oh ! that's her niece, or rather, must be her husband's niece, as her name is Trafford too. I rather fancy Mrs Traff' takes it out of her."

"I shouldn't wonder· at all. She's marvellously good-looking."

"Think so ? Never saw her in that light myself. Of course, she's very superior to Mrs Traff's style, which is a very shabby sort, tea-pot spout about the nose, and *very* shady about the feet. I must say," Crecy went on, being blessed with an exceedingly free and voluble tongue, "I must say I do like a woman, no matter what her age or class, to be tidy about her feet: there's something demoralising about feet that don't tread true and boots that get bulgy. Don't you think so ? "

"Yes ; true," with a laugh. "I didn't happen to look at her feet, but I'll be sworn they're all right."

"They are. I happen to have looked at them a good many times, and could swear to them anywhere. You may take my word for

it, there isn't a smarter or a prettier pair of
steppers in the whole town, or, for the matter
of that, out of it. But, all the same, I don't
know that I ever heard her called good-looking
before. Still, these things are all pretty much
a matter of taste," in a careless tone, as he
stopped at the door of a shop, in the window
of which there was a fine display of ties and
cape driving-gloves. "I want to go in here.
Do you mind?"

"Not at all," answered Orford.

So the two men passed into the shop,
and Orford stood staring meditatively out of
the door, while Crecy bought some odds and
ends which he would want on the march, and
paid his bill. But though he was apparently
so engrossed in watching the people go up
and down the street, Marcus Orford saw in
reality nothing but the face of the girl whom
he and Crecy had passed ten minutes before—
the girl who was niece to the little pushing
person whom Crecy called "Mrs Traff."

And then, when Crecy informed him that
he had finished his business and was ready
to depart, he shook himself free of his reflec-
tions, and remembered that he had come off
march *minus* a hat of any kind, excepting his
best go-to-meeting stove-pipe. Then, having
bought himself a hat and some gloves and
ties, he said that was all he wanted, and was
ready to go wherever Crecy chose to take him.

So the two went swinging up the street together, a noticeable pair, because Crecy was a general favourite with all sorts and conditions of men at Blankhampton —men *and* women that is — and Marcus Orford, still wearing his undress uniform, was a man whom nobody at any time could or would be likely or willing to overlook

For a finer fellow than Marcus Orford it seldom falls to the lot of any commanding officer to welcome into his regiment, either as officer or as a simple trooper. He was big and broad and strong, with a firm, free, swaggering gait, and yet a swagger that was pleasant to look upon, and entirely free from aught that could offend. And not only was he of fine and stalwart person, but he was handsome of face, with a happy, hearty laugh, and a pair of eyes that were simply killing, as grey as a tabby cat—eyes that when they were not dancing with fun could put on a die-away look which women found irresistible.

Was it any wonder that the fair damsels of Blankhampton, recognising that Crecy's companion was one of the new officers, bestowed smiles upon him which were even more sweet than usual, and gave him pleased lingering little bows which said plainly enough, "Oh! do stop and tell us who that handsome fellow is ?"

But if Crecy saw what the smiles and the

bows meant he remained blind to what they were intended to convey. There are none so blind, you know, as those who won't see, and Crecy, if it suited him to be so, could be as blind as any bat.

So they went on together, stopping at several shops, and finally just looking into the club, which, as everybody who has been in Blankhampton knows, stands just opposite to the principal entrance to the Winter Garden, and scarcely more than a stone's-throw from the edifice which Blankhampton folk familiarly call "the Parish," but which, nevertheless, is the pride of the county, and one of the purest and noblest specimens of Gothic architecture to be found in the length and breadth of Europe.

They did not stop there many minutes, only, in fact, just long enough for Crecy to introduce Orford to one or two men of the neighbourhood whom they happened to find there, for Crecy had a good deal yet to do in the matter of looking after his belongings, and had very little time to do it in.

"Will you go back with me, or would you rather stop here and come back later?" he asked Orford.

"I'll go back," said Orford promptly. He had taken rather a fancy to his new acquaintance, and willingly left Blankhampton magnates to take care of themselves; that he would.

sooner or later, know all about them was quite
a matter of course.

"Fine house that," he remarked, as they
turned the corner of the street in which the
club was situate; "but what a display of arms."

"The Mayor's house; his official residence,"
Crecy explained. "The Mansion House they
call it, of course."

"H—m! I suppose the Mayor's an awful
swell?"

"Oh! something too awful! Queer thing;
but the office carries the dignity of knighthood
with it. I don't know exactly why. Some
Mayor of Blankhampton or other saved somebody's life; Charles the Second, I believe; can't
say for certain, but anyway, the first thing a
man does when he gets made Mayor of Blankhampton is to bundle off to Windsor or Balmoral
or Osborne, or anywhere that her Majesty
happens to be, and he gets made Sir Thomas
or John or George, as the case may be. Odd
study of human nature they make, those same
Sir Thomases and Johns and Georges, and my
ladies are odder still. Can't say if it's true,
I'm sure, but they do say that one old girl
is greater fun than all the rest put together."

"Titles must be as plentiful as blackberries on
a bramble-bush," laughed Orford.

"Yes; and it's very funny when you go to
call on any of them for a solemn servant to
inform you, 'My lady is at 'ome,' and for my

lady to inform you that the glass is gone *hup !*
One gets used to it in time, but the effect is
distinctly funny at first."

"Yes, must be very funny," Orford answered :
then, his grey eyes having spied out a face he
had seen before, just within the door of a big
bookseller's shop, he added, " Oh ! by-the-bye, I
want some pencils.   Do you mind coming in
with me ?   I sha'n't be above a minute or two."

He went straight into the shop, followed by
Crecy, who found himself as soon as he entered
almost in the arms of Mrs Trafford.   That lady
greeted him with effusion, with a display of
feeling most of anything like a mother wel-
coming back a long-lost child.

" My *dear* Mr Crecy," she exclaimed, " I quite
thought we had seen the last of you !   *When*
do you go ? "

" Leave to-morrow morning," Crecy answered.

" Oh! *really !* We shall all be *so* sorry to
lose you.   Could you not come in for a cup of
tea ?   For the very *last* time ? "

" Oh ! thanks.   I—I—" Crecy was beginning
in civil refusal, when he felt his arm seized from
behind and vigorously pinched.

" Introduce me," said Orford, in his ear.

" Certainly. Mrs Trafford, may I introduce
Mr Orford, one of the new regiment ? "

Mrs Trafford said, " With pleasure," and Orford, after the manner of his class, said, " How
d'you do ? "

"Do come back and have a cup of tea. We are going straight home," Mrs Trafford urged.

"We shall be delighted," said Orford, in utter and blissful disregard of the fact that Crecy was really and truly pressed for time.

"That is right. My daughter—my niece, Mr Orford. Now, Mr Crecy, will you walk with me?"

So Crecy, very much against his will, had to escort Mrs Trafford up the High Street, while Orford followed with the daughter—a very counterpart of her mother, nose and all; but, to his unutterable chagrin and disgust, Mrs Trafford kept tight hold of her niece's arm.

"Downy old cat!" said Orford, in high wrath to himself. "I'll be even with her for this."

However, wrath or not wrath, he had to be civil to the young lady, who made herself very friendly and pleasant as they went along the street in quite a little procession.

They passed Mrs Hugh on the road, who fairly boiled over with disgust when she saw the clever capture that "that horrid little hag" had made. "In uniform, too!" said Mrs Hugh to her own soul in righteous indignation. "Really, I wonder the off-icers *can* tolerate her; but it shows what push can do."

If she had only known how sick within them were the souls of the two off-icers; how one was being dragged along utterly against his will and as a matter of pure choice would rather have been talking to Polly at that moment than to any other woman in the whole of Blankhampton; and how the other had been cleverly planted on to a girl with whom he would, if left to himself, almost as soon as thought of jumping off the tower of "the Parish" as of escorting down the High Street, why, without doubt, Mrs Hugh's disgusted soul would have been considerably mollified.

However, unfortunately for her, she did not know it, and so went on her way seething and swelling with envy, hatred, and all uncharitable-ness. Ay, but Mrs Hugh was just on the eve of a most humiliating discovery, one that was just beginning to dawn upon her—it was that a lovely face, with what she was pleased to call a cold manner, has not a ghost of a chance against a pert little teapot spout with plenty of push.

Ay, di mi! It is a sad thing that in this world there is nothing like push for securing the plums out of the pudding; nothing like push for getting yourself into the best places of fashion's raree show; nothing like push for getting, in short, the best of everything.

And there were people in Blankhampton ill-natured enough to say without hesitation, that the fair Polly was neither more nor less than as stupid as an owl.

SIDELIGHT.

THE HONOURABLE MARCUS ORFORD.

HE happened to be staying in a country house, where the game-bag formed so considerable part of a not very large revenue, that only men with the reputation of being very good shots were ever asked to the shooting-parties.

It was the first time he had ever been invited to the house, and, unfortunately, the first time he went out with the guns, he found himself in wretched form.

"Tut-tut," muttered his host at the first miss.

"Bless my soul," he remarked at the second.

"T-ta! There goes seven-and-sixpence!" he exclaimed, as a fine cock pheasant got off scot-free.

Marcus Orford would like to have twisted the old gentleman's neck for him. However, nettled though he was, such a course was not open to him, so he waited till a soft furry little bunny popped across the path in front of them, and then he called out at the top of his loud and healthy voice,—

"Hi! Sir Thomas! Sir Thomas! there goes eighteen pence. Take care you don't miss him!"

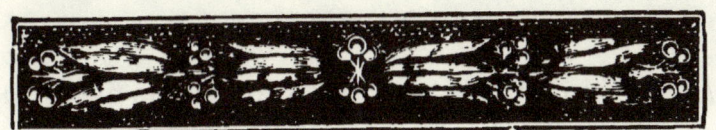

CHAPTER IV.

CLASS DISTINCTIONS.

MARCUS ORFORD very soon found that Mrs Traff, as she seemed very generally to be called, was not the only person of push—or daughters—in Blankhampton. He was now an officer of nearly seven years' service, but his lot had never been cast in a Blankhampton before. The only approach to it had been Warnecliffe, where the rush of mothers and daughters had been mere child's play compared with this new experience.

There is an old jingle much in vogue among little ladies still in the schoolroom which says,—

> "Tinker;
> Tailor;
> Soldier;
> Sailor;
> Rich man;
> Poor man;
> Beggar man;
> Thief!"

And, I think, if we take exception to the first two
on the list and add a second and similar jingle
thereto, which says,—

> " Army ;
> Navy ;
> Church ;
> Law,"

we shall have a very fair idea of the different sorts and conditions of folk, who, not
perhaps altogether unnaturally, thought that
Lord Ceespring's only son would make a very
pleasant and desirable addition to their family ;
for, besides the soldiers and the sailors, the rich
men and the poor men, and the rest, he found a
large and varied assortment of the clerical and
legal professions all willing, even eager, to enter
the lists and scramble for him

It was astonishing how many men in the
neighbourhood had been at Eton or at Oxford
with his father, and how many ladies had danced
in the same room or employed the same dressmaker as his beautiful mother; it was astonishing, and yet it was perhaps not astonishing
at all, for everybody, not only around, but actually *in* Blankhampton, claimed to be something very superior to all their fellows—as if
they were real diamonds, which had got quite
by accident into an assortment of paste.

After the manner of most men, Marcus
Orford was in the habit of sticking his cards
of invitation into the little space between the

plate and the gilt frame of his chimney-glass, which, as in the rooms of most officers, was the most noticeable feature in his quarters. In other quarters he had been accustomed to put visiting-cards on one side of the glass, and invitation cards on the other: but when he was fairly settled and known at Blank-hampton, he very soon found the accommodation utterly inadequate, for cards and notes came upon him so thick and fast that before long he had to set up a bowl for cards, visiting-cards, that is, so as to leave the other side of the tall glass at liberty for those of invitation.

They were an odd assortment, and varied from the large and solemn-looking card stamped with the arms of the city in scarlet and gold, which bade him to the pompous banquet of three hundred covers, to the gushing note, fragrant with Ess. Bouquet, which coaxingly invited him to dine in *quite* a friendly way, which, being interpreted, meant the usual seven courses and ice pudding, but with guests in the proportion of two to four, two ladies—mother and daughter; or from the plain card which summoned him to the episcopal garden party to Mrs Traff's—" *Won't* you come in after 'the Parish' on Sunday afternoon ? "

A good many of Mrs Traff's little notes found their way into the Cavalry Barracks in the course of the year, but Marcus Orford

received far more of them than was his share,
if he and the other officers of the Black Horse
had gone on the share-and-share-alike principle.

As a general rule, Mrs Traff found that the
sending forth of her little notes was something like fishing for trout on a bright
summer's day with a blue sky overhead; but
when Marcus Orford received the first one,
and wrote back that he should be delighted
to avail himself of her invitation, Mrs Traff
began to think that she had got a nibble from
a fish at last that only needed a little patience
and perseverance to land successfully.

" He is such a nice fellow, you know, dears,"
said Mrs Traff, to her daughters, when Marcus
Orford's note arrived. " We must really try
and make the place a little pleasant to him ;
there are so few *nice* people here. I nev-ah ! "
she added, in a reflective tone, as she poised her
teaspoon with great care on the edge of her
coffee cup, " I never go anywhere in Blankhampton without feeling that really the society
of the place is *ve-ry* limited. I never thought
it would be such a pushing sort of place. I
quite fancied that, being a cathedral town and
all that, that society would be more select.
But really only the Parish set is at all exclusive, and really that is not as particular as
could be wished. Dear Lady Margaret thinks
so little of class distinctions, which is a great
mistake · by being so—so—open-hearted, she

saddles herself and the dear Dean with a great many undesirable acquaintances," which was true enough, Mrs Traff' among the number.

"Oh, it's Lady Margaret's 'form' to know everybody in the place," said the younger Miss Traff', who was a really pretty girl, and called Laura.

"Must be a great bore knowing so many common sort of people," commented Mrs Traff' with her nose in the air—I mean more in the air than Nature had put it. "I must say I never saw the force or use of doing it. Even before I was married to your dear father, when I took my position in the county as the adopted daughter of Miss Spillman of Hollow Spell, I was always most particular about the people I knew. Madge, what are you laughing at?" she asked sharply, suddenly addressing her niece, with an utter change of tone.

Madge Trafford laughed outright.

"I was thinking how furiously that fat old lady looked at you the other day when we were walking up the High Street with Mr Orford and Mr Crecy."

"Oh, yes; I daresay. You mean *that* Mrs Antrobus?"

"Yes! An enormously stout old lady with a benign smile."

"And a lovely daughter," put in Laura, who was a regular little firebrand, and loved to see her energetic mother flare up.

"Lovely! Yes, if you admire that dairymaid type," with great scorn.

"Dairymaid! I wish I was of the dairymaid type then," cried Laura. "Don't you, Madge?"

"I think she's one of the prettiest girls in the town," replied Madge promptly.

"Pretty! What nonsense! She's lovely— such eyes, such a lovely nose, such lips, such teeth, *and* SUCH a *heavenly* skin," Laura persisted.

"And such a mother," added Mrs Traff, in all the consciousness of proud superiority. "Such an absurd woman—aspiring to know the army people, when 'the Parish' set would as soon know the dustman at once. So absurd! Mrs Wingham was telling me all about her the other day; and really the poor woman seems to have made a complete fool of herself. She has an idea that her pretty pink and white daughter is going to make a great match, and thinks knowing the officers will bring it about."

"Miss Antrobus was engaged to Eliot Cardella, anyway," put in Madge quietly.

"So Mrs Wingham says, at least she says that the Antrobuses wished it to be believed so, but the Mallinbros very soon stopped all that; and then she made herself foolish by a great display of intimacy with Mrs Trelawney. Mrs Wingham declares that she positively didn't know that Mrs Trelawney was not known in society, and cut her dead as soon as she found it out; so silly, as if Mrs Trelawney would have been intimate with *her* if she had been all right."

"But you couldn't expect Mrs Antrobus to believe or admit that," laughed Julia Trafford, who was a later edition of her mother, nose and cracked voice and all.

"But it is true," cried Mrs Traff' shrilly. "I must say I detest such stupid pushing ways For my own part," she added, laying the palms of her hands together, and tapping the tips of her fingers one against another, "I have *no* wish to rise socially."

Of course not. At that time Mrs Traff's object was not to encompass the impossible and rise in the social scale, but to set about making Blankhampton as pleasant as possible to Lord Ceespring's only son, and particularly that part of it which was printed in various colours underneath a smart crest at the head of her note-paper—7, *St Eve's, Blankhampton.*

With this object in view she set about getting a lot of people together after the Parish on Sunday afternoon.

"Dear Mrs Cornwallis," she said to the wife of a general—a major-general, that is—on the staff; "do come in and have a cup of tea after the Parish on Sunday."

"Very sorry," said Mrs Cornwallis, without the faintest trace of sorrow in her tone, "but

we have promised to go in to the Mauleverers;
they're expecting some of the new regiment."

"So are we," smiled Mrs Traff.' "What
a pity. I am so grieved. I was just going
to ask the Mauleverers to come. I am always
so unfortunate with them. You see we live
so near together that we almost invariably ask
people on the same days."

"Yes, the Parish and the Winter Garden
are your two great assemblies, are they not?"
said the wife of the general civilly.

"Yes, they are. Well, good-bye. I hope
you'll come to us another Sunday," smiling
still.

"Thanks, very much; but we are going away
for two months' leave on Monday; perhaps
when we come back. Good-bye."

"Good-bye," returned Mrs Traff.' "Good-
bye."

She was a plucky little woman—as little
sharp-nosed women often are—and she smiled
bravely into Mrs Cornwallis's eyes to the last.
But oh, *what* a rage she was in; for the name
of Mauleverer fairly stank in her nostrils, and
the mention of it was intolerable to her.

For though by dint of plenty of push (and
a not small amount of what the young people
of the present day call cheek, together with a
fair share of that thickness of skin and fre-
quent lack of moral perception which are the
first and most essential necessaries for persons

who wish to get into a social sphere in which
they were not born), she had managed to push
her way into "the Parish" set, and among
the army people , yet the Mauleverers —
four middle-aged "spins," who still kept up
the fiction of requiring a chaperon—would have
none of her; and to Mrs Traff' they stood pre-
cisely in the same place that Mordecai did to
Haman as he sat in the king's gate.

Mrs Traff' was simply furious: these ancient
damsels were skinny and plain and withered;
they had never been much to look at, being
of that pre-eminently aristocratic type which
looks like a good sort of geranium very much
run to seed. But if they were skinny and
gaunt and all that, they were nearly related
to most of the best families in the county,
and they did not take kindly to Mrs Traff'.
In fact, they would not have her at any price;
and no matter how high did this modern and
feminine edition of Haman rise, these daughters
of Mordecai bowed not, nor did her reverence.

However, in spite of her failure to secure
Mrs Cornwallis—who, though the wife of a
major-general, was a young and very lovely
woman, being thirty and odd years younger
than her husband—Mrs Traff' did scrape together
a very fair show of people for the following
Sunday afternoon.

There was the beautiful daughter of the
handsome Dean—"dear Lady Margaret" having

gone home to get forty winks wherewith to refresh herself—who looked somewhat wearied, as if she was not quite sure whether her back ached or the company bored her the most. And there was the latest bride, with her husband, a retired general, small and man-of-the-world-like, yet a very fair sort of bridegroom for a bride who was neither young nor bonny, nor even pleasant-looking, and apparently had had nothing but a little money to recommend her. And there was the bride's aunt, a tall, grenadier-like lady in weeds, possessed with an idea, which seemed to be ineradicable, that she was the squire of Blankhampton.

"Who's this funny old party?" asked Marcus Orford of Colonel Coles, the most good-natured and inveterate gossip in the whole of the garrison.

"Oh, that's Mrs Forster," answered the Colonel, as if the information was sufficient in itself to fully enlighten Orford's curiosity.

"Mrs Forster. Ah! and who was the blest departed before he shuffled off this mortal coil?"

Colonel Coles laughed outright.

"Not a bad little chap—gentleman and all that—but sadly overshadowed by his bigger-half. They say she used to bully him fearfully—in fact," lowering his voice to a discreet whisper, "of course I can't say if it's true, but Hardy—of Crow Nest, you know—assured me as a positive thing that his butler, who came to

him from the Forsters, declared that he never
wished to serve a better master than little
Forster was, ' But,' he said, ' I couldn't stand
that devil any longer.' "

" She was a nobody, you know," Colonel
Coles went on. " Father was a policeman, or
something of that sort. I suppose Forster
thought her a fine woman when he married
her, poor little chap."

" H—m, must have repented himself of the
evil pretty often afterwards," laughed Orford.

" I believe you! You never happened to
see her in church, did you ? "

" Saw her this afternoon."

" Oh, yes ; but I mean in St Bavon's—her
own church ? No! Ah! it's a great joke.
You know this dean — Adair — hasn't been
here very long, and the old dean, who, by-
the-bye, was a Cardella, had an old-fashioned
way of answering all the responses in church
just a shade in front of the choir. He had
a little, thin, reedy voice, and the effect was
something like this,—

" O—Lord, open Thou our Lips.
     And our mouth shall——
         And our Mou—th shall shew
           for—th Thy Praise !

" It didn't sound bad in him, but with Mrs
Forster it is thus,—

" O—God—make speed to save us.
O Lord make haste to help us.
O Lord—make haste to help us. .

" You can hear her all over the church;
I assure you it's the funniest thing in creation. Ah, there's Mrs Fairlie ! I must go
and speak to her: prettiest woman in Blankhampton ; quite the Mrs Langtry of the place;
introduce you, if you like."

" Thanks, many; no, I—er—don't seem to
care about it. Not much in my line, you
know."

" Perhaps so: pretty woman though, and
great fun too."

" Ah, I should quite think so," returned
Orford.

So Colonel Coles moved off to pay his
respects to Mrs Fairlie, who was the very
vain wife of a professional man, and formed
a connecting link between the cathedral set,
which was somewhat exclusive, and the class
among whom Mrs Hugh was, so to speak, a
great and shining light.

And then Mrs Traff', seeing her most valued
guest standing alone, set about trying to make
the afternoon " a little pleasant" to him ; and
by dint of paying him a good deal of attention herself, and then by making him acquainted with Miss Laura, her youngest
flower, and by reminding him that he had

not seen Miss Julia, she contrived to succeed
so well that he never, from first to last,
had the very smallest chance of saying a
single word to the girl for whose sake, and
for the sake of whose *beaux yeux* he had—
to use his own graphic, if not strictly elegant
words—let himself in for all *that* lot.

"He's such a *nice* fellow," cried Mrs Traff'
in an ecstasy to her young ladies, as she
watched him, the last to depart of all her
guests, go across the street, "and stayed such
a *long* time."

If she had only known why he stayed so
long !

SIDELIGHT.

COLONEL COLES.

 LITTLE American lady once watched the old Colonel for a long time, then put a pretty, dainty head on one side till her mouth reached the ear of a friend sitting by.

"I think that old gentleman fancies himself," she said simply.

It was true; he did fancy himself in many ways, but most of all as a judge of old china and such-like. Generally he got taken in finely —two chips and a little dirt being sufficient for the purpose—although the stuff might be as new as potatoes in May.

But once the two Damerel girls laid their fair heads together and literally cooked a piece of porcelain for him, to the joy and delight of a large circle of admiring friends and acquaintances. First they got a nice saucer of plain white paste all ready for painting purposes, this they carefully decorated from a selection of Lady Mainwaring's china cabinet, including choice specimens of Lowestoft, Chelsea, Sevres, and Crown-Derby, while underneath they carefully painted the Bow mark in vermilion; when finished, they sent it to be baked, then they added a great deal of gold, and had it baked again. Then they contrived two careful chips, which they stained brown with a decoction of Spanish juice, and a great deal of dirt, after which they asked for his opinion upon it.

The Colonel turned it over and over, held it up to the light, wetted his finger and rubbed the mark very clean, held it at arm's length, and looked at the mark again.

"A very rare specimen," he said at length, "of Newcastle!" which repaid their trouble and made their triumph complete.

CHAPTER V.

"THE GATE OF PARADISE."

"CAROLINE MAINWARING," said Marcus Orford aloud, as he reached the end of a short and effusive note one morning soon after Mrs Traff's pleasant afternoon after "the Parish"—at least, I mean the afternoon which she had endeavoured to make a little pleasant to him. "Now who in the wide world, I wonder, is 'Caroline Mainwaring'?"

"Caroline Mainwaring!" repeated that inveterate gossip Colonel Coles, who had just put his beaming old face into the Black Horse mess in order to pick up any flotsam and jetsam in the shape of gossip which might happen to be floating about. "Why, Lady Mainwaring, of course."

"And who is Lady Mainwaring? One of the Sir Thomases' or Johns' or Georges' wives?"

"Oh, dear no! quite a different being. She's widow of Sir Albert Mainwaring, who built the big bridge over the channel."

"Oh! really. H—m! What does she want to write to me for? *I* don't know the woman. 'My dear Mr Orford.' Ah! one has a pretty fair idea of what a woman one doesn't know is after when she writes, 'My *dear* Mr Orford,' and signs herself, 'Yours *very* truly.' Eh, Colonel?"

"Yes!" growled Urquhart. "I had one the other day. I suppose she's got a daughter to marry. Ugh! Nice sort of husband I should make for her."

"I've no doubt, sir," put in Lester Brookes, with a laugh, "that Lady Mainwaring thinks you would make the best of husbands. She thought I might do at a pinch, until she found out I was not one of the Lancashire Brookeses. 'Your dear mother and I, Mr Brookes,' she said to me the other day, 'were girls together; we played with dolls together went to school together, went to the same balls, the same picnics, the same dressmaker. So we must be good friends, must we not? And you are *so* like her; just the same look across the eyes,' and then she made a telescope of a very skinny hand with a lot of diamond rings upon it, and made me feel, hang it, as uncomfortable as if I was getting photographed.

"'I remember,' she went on, 'ages and ages ago, before ever I met dear Sir Albert, or your mother had even thought of marriage at all, that your grandfather, dear old Mr Armytage, gave a party for her and—'

"I broke in then," Brookes went on, "and told her that it couldn't have been the same, as my mother was a Ramsay, and that my grandfather, I believed, died when she was six weeks old.

"'Oh! then,' she said, 'you are not one of the Lancashire Brookeses?'

"'No,' said I. 'I am not in any way related to the Lancashire Brookeses.' And," he went on, "it is astonishing how little interest Lady Mainwaring has taken in me since."

"Turned her attention to you, Colonel, eh?" cried Orford, with a laugh. "Fine case of dropping the substance for the shadow, wasn't it? Well, I don't feel inclined to help her ladyship off with her daughters myself, but I shall make it my business on the very first opportunity to let her know that Pitch-and-Toss here is better worth her while to look after than you are. Seems such a pity for a nice old lady to be wasting powder and shot over the most inveterate bachelor in the service, when there is a nice young man like Pitch-and-Toss literally going begging. By-the-bye, what are the daughters like?"

"There are no daughters," answered the

gossip Coles, "but there are two nieces pretty enough to make a man's mouth water."

"Two nieces — the devil! And what may they be called?"

"Their names are Damerel — Margaret and Elizabeth Damerel. They stay here a good deal. I think their home is in the West of Ireland somewhere."

"Oh! and the old lady wants to get rid of them," was Orford's nice comment. "Well, as I said, I don't feel inclined to help her off myself, but I haven't the least objection to putting her on the right road for all that. But I wonder how she comes to know me? I never met her that I know of. Never was introduced to her; that I'll swear."

"Oh, she was at school with your mother," cried Brookes, with a laugh.

"Not unlikely. My poor mother has been at school with so many good ladies about Blankhampton that it's not at all improbable. My mother says herself she never was at school; but that, of course, is only a detail."

"By-the-bye," from the Colonel, as the laugh which followed Orford's words died away, "Brookes, did you not promise to look at that colley pup with me this afternoon?"

"Yes, sir, I did."

"Then will you come round to my quarters presently?"

"Certainly, sir."

"Half-an-hour hence will do. I have some papers to look over first. Good morning, Coles."

"Morning, Colonel," returned Coles cheerfully; and then, as the door of the ante-room closed upon Urquhart's departing figure, the babel of voices broke out again, and gossip waxed more fast and furious than ever.

"What pup's that, Brookes?" asked Orford.

"One he wants for Mrs Traff'," Brookes replied.

"One—he—wants—for—MRS—TRAFF'!" Orford repeated, in slow and astounded accents, and with an expression of countenance as if he were not sure whether his own headpiece had suddenly gone wrong or whether Brookes' wits were "sweet bells jangled out of tune." "*What* did you say, Brookes?"

"Say? I said he wanted it for Mrs Traff'," Brookes answered, grinning.

"The Colonel?"

"Yes."

"*Urquhart?*" Orford persisted.

"Yes, Urquhart," replied Brookes, laughing outright.

"Are you sure?"

"As sure as I am that you are the most headlong dare-devil in the whole of the service."

Orford's astonishment was so great that he actually forgot to shy his forage-cap or anything else at his informant; instead, he shook his head with solemn portent.

"I'll tell you what it is," he said gravely. "It's a pitiable thing when a rattling good fellow such as Urquhart used to be goes in for the heavy father style of business, but when he goes on and on till he starts getting colley pups for Mrs Traffs—well, then, I think it's about time for his friends to interfere and put a stop to it."

"Which of them is it?" asked Coles, who saw nothing particularly improbable in the commanding officer of the Black Horse being strongly attracted to the pretty house in St Eve's.

"Which of them is it?" cried Orford; "why Mrs Traff' herself, of course. You don't suppose the Colonel would make a mother-in-law of her, do you? Good heavens! there'd be no holding her!"

"There's the niece," returned the gossip mildly.

"The niece," sharply. "Oh! pooh, nonsense; it's absurd on the very face of it."

"Always thought her an uncommonly good-looking girl myself," said the old gossip calmly. "By-the-bye, haven't you a fellow who writes?"

"We can all read and write, thank God," returned St Maur piously.

"Yes, yes, but I mean novels and so on."

"Ye-s. Devilish good ones too: but he's on

leave just now; broke his leg some time back,
and it don't mend quite so well as it should.
Good chap, too, and as clever as daylight."

" What's his name ? "

" Murphy ; Irish fellow ; you may have heard
the name before."

" Yes, but not as an author," Coles declared.

St Maur laughed.

"Sounds grand that, eh, Orford? an au-thor !
Yes ; but he writes devilish good yarns, devilish
good ; uses the name of Tempest. Fine name
Tempest, as we often tell him. We call him
' the Wind ' for short."

" But he has made a great hit with that thing
of his, *The Gate of Paradise*," Coles cried.

" Of course he has ; devilish good story it is
too. As I often tell him, having gone up like
a rocket, let us pray the Almighty he does not
end by coming down like a stick."

" I suppose he has made a pot of money ? "

" Oh, ah—so so—pretty fair, I believe ; means
to do big things, of course. Ah ! Went to see
him in town the other day when I was up ;
found him in a fearful rage. Yes, he is rather
an excitable sort of chap, can't stand meanness
of any sort. It seems he wanted to give a copy
of *The Gate of Paradise* to a certain gifted
authoress, who had been to see him in his im-
prisonment, so he wrote a civil line to his publishers saying that he should be awfully obliged,
don't you know, if they would send him one or

two cloth copies of the book. Just the same as
the shilling book, you know, only it sells at half-
a-crown, and is bound in red cloth.

"Well, as the book had been a big success, and
the publishing fellows had got it, so to speak,
for an old song, poor old Wind simply, as I said,
asked for one or two, and, if you'll believe me,
they sent 'em, and with 'em a bill—a—bill—

	s.	d.
"Two cloth copies of *The Gate of Paradise*, 1s. 9d., .	3	6
Postage, ...	0	6
Total, . .	4	0

"Of course he was in an awful rage about it,
as any fellow would be, but I really do think it
was the 'Postage, 6d.' that cut the poor old chap
up so fearfully. I don't believe, if they had just
said

"Two cloth copies of
The Gate of Paradise, 2s. 6d.—5s.,

that he'd have taken it half so badly.

"However, poor chap, he entered into a long
and moving account of how, *after* he had
signed the agreement to sell *The Gate of Paradise* to these people, they found out that it
was just a shade short, and begged him to add
a little to it. And, poor old boy, he actually
wrote a whole chapter—that one about the

Married Woman's Property Act—and sent it to them, without ever dreaming of asking a penny for it. Gad, I can tell you his remarks on the subject were worth hearing, they were as spicy as the balmy breezes we hear about on missionary Sundays. And by way of revenging himself, and making his wrongs known to the world, he's got the blessed old bill itself nicely framed and glazed, and has it hung up where he can keep it well in view, both for himself and everyone who goes to see him.

"'What the devil's that?' said I, as soon as I went into his room—for, you know, 'tis about the most conspicuous object on any of the four walls.

"And then, poor old chap, he told me all about it, and, 'pon my word, I really thought he'd have burst with rage and fury long before he had got to the end of his tale.

"' *I* wouldn't worry, old man,' said I; 'didn't some fellow or other say, "Barabbas was a publisher"?'

"'You mean "Judas Iscariot,"' he screamed, 'Why, Barabbas was a decent, honest man compared with—' but just then the doctor turned up for his daily visit, and as I thought somehow he looked better able to bear the brunt of the storm than I—I came away and left him to the full enjoyment of it."

"About the best thing you could do," old Coles laughed. "It's never the smallest use arguing with a man who has a grievance, and it's a great bore hearing him out to the bitter end."

"That is so," St Maur answered; "that certainly is so. And if I were you, I should just keep out of the Wind's way after he first gets back again, for if he's enlarged and beautified and touched up that story as he does some service yarns that appear in print, why, it will be a veritable case of 'The wind bloweth where it listeth: no man can tell whence it cometh, nor whither it goeth.' For my part, I have every intention of picking a quarrel with him the day after he rejoins."

"I don't think I shall," said Orford, more as if he were thinking aloud than speaking for the benefit of the public at large.

"Then Marcus is brewing some extra devilment in the form of a practical joke," muttered Brookes—then added aloud, "Well, time's up for the Chief—I must be off."

"And that special Providence," Marcus Orford called after him with sententious piety, "which watches over the fortunes of children, drunkards, and fools, go with you."

"Thank you," returned Brookes, with unction; "I'll tell the Chief of your solicitude for his welfare."

"I say, Colonel," said Orford to the gossip when the door had closed with a bang behind Brookes, who went - out with considerable

acceleration of speed in order to avoid a missile
in the shape of Debrett's *Peerage* which Orford
had sent flying across the room at him; " do
you happen to know if Mrs Traff' is a friend of
Lady Mainwaring ? "

" I rather fancy she is, or perhaps, literally
speaking, Mrs Traff' claims Lady Mainwaring
as a great friend of hers."

" If I go to this tea thing, is there any chance
of the Traffs being there ? "

" I can't say, I'm sure. I certainly have seen
them there."

" H—m ! Well, I think I shall go," in the
thinking-aloud tone again.

" Which of them is it ? " the old gossip asked
inquisitively—so inquisitively that Orford saw
he had made a slip.

" Well, you see Urquhart and I are old
chums, and if he's got such a bee in his bonnet
as to be thinking of Mrs Traff', why, I'll do my
best to keep his eyes open for him, just for
auld sake's sake, you know."

" How deuced philanthropic you've got all
of a sudden, Markey," exclaimed Archie Falconer, who had just entered in time to hear
his comrade's answer. " Urquhart ought to
be awfully obliged to you."

Orford turned quickly round, and stretched
out his hand eagerly.

" Why, Archie, when did you come back ? I
didn't know you were coming for ages yet."

"Yes, leave's up to-day."

"And how's Lady Archie?"

"She's very well indeed, thanks — all the better for her trip. And how do you like this place?"

"It's not half bad. By-the-bye, you haven't met Colonel Coles, have you?"

"No, I haven't. How do you do?" Lord Archie answered. "Ah! how d'you do, Hastings? Why, you look very seedy, old chap — been ill?"

"Oh! no, no — I'm all right, thanks!" Hastings answered, but, all the same, though he might be all right, yet at the sight of his comrade he had grown white to the very lips: then, by an intense effort he asked, "How is Lady Archie?"

"Oh, quite well, thanks; as blooming as possible, and all the better for her trip to Norway. You'll come and see her, of course?"

"Oh, thanks; I shall be delighted," Hastings answered, without the slightest inflection of delight in his voice.

His memory, for the matter of that, had gone back too keenly to feel any delight at the prospect of seeing Lady Archie Falconer again, to a lonely grave over by the Red Sea in sun-scorched Suakim, a grave in which was lying the only woman who had ever loved him — a woman whose heart he had broken; yes, broken!

Oh, how his mind went back to it all again, to the last time he had seen it—

To the Blessed Memory

of

ELIZABETH LANGLEY

(*Sister Myra*),

Her Britannic Majesty's Nursing Staff,

Who Died at her post on the 9th of April, During the British campaign of 1885.

"Faithful unto Death."

He turned sharply round and went straight out of the room, leaving Lord Archie staring after him open-mouthed.

"What is it?" he asked of the others.

"Oh! don't take any notice, poor old chap," answered Austin. "I daresay your turning up so suddenly after your long leave reminded him of Sister Myra. Poor old Hastings has never been the same since the awful morning he turned round and found her sitting dead beside him. She'd been awfully good to him, and Hastings declared she was the only woman he had ever loved; raved frantically that he had murdered her; in fact, went off his head altogether, and had a bad go of brain fever over it. I suppose he really wasn't very far out of it in saying he murdered her, though, of course, poor chap, he couldn't help it. But I do think she pulled Hastings through that enteric fever at the cost of her own life. I don't think there can be any doubt of that. Anyway, Alban has never been the same man since, and I remember perfectly that he was as lively as a cricket only the day before, for I went on board the hospital ship on purpose to see him."

"I didn't even know Sister Myra was dead!" Lord Archie exclaimed. "She nursed me when I was wounded, you know. By Jove! but that was a woman; her patience was inexhaustible."

And then Lord Archie stopped to reflect, to recall what had never struck him very forcibly before—that Sister Myra's patience and tenderness had not been so much for him as for that other one who lay in the next cot raving about the Lent lilies and the aconites at home, and the lilies of the valley which strayed into the lawn turf, and how "Father mowed them down—"

"Did Hastings know her before?" he asked abruptly.

"Yes; she came from his own place. I believe they had been children together."

"And she died beside him. Ah! I wonder—" and then Lord Archie broke off short, remembering that it is best to let sleeping dogs lie, and dead ones fade out of memory altogether; yet, in his own mind he made a guess at the truth that day which was right in the centre of the bull's eye.

SIDELIGHT.

LADY MAINWARING.

IN the town her ladyship invariably gave herself the airs of a patron! And one day she happened to go into the shop of a silk mercer, one of those old-fashioned establishments only to be found in county towns, where the master is always to be seen about the premises.

Lady Mainwaring was not a *good* customer; in fact, she got most of her gowns from London, and patronised this particular shop for odds and ends. On this occasion she bought enough of these to amount to two and fourpence half-penny, to pay which she laid on the counter a half-crown.

The salesman gave her a little bill, and the change in copper, a penny half-penny.

"Are you offering copper to *me?*" demanded my lady.

The salesman explained that her change was to the amount of one penny half-penny.

"I never heard of such a thing as to take the coppers—not another shop in Blankhampton would dream of such a thing!" my lady cried.

He said he was very sorry they could not afford to take fourpence half-penny off so small a sum.

She promptly asked for the master, and appealed to him, but the master was firm.

"Our Mr Smith has been with us fifteen years, my lady," said he; "and if he says we cannot afford it, I am quite sure we cannot."

"Then I'll never enter your shop again!" she exclaimed, and stalked to the door.

"John," said the silk mercer, as she reached it; "John, you'd better put the shutters up!"

CHAPTER VI.

BOLTED!

WHEN the day of Lady Mainwaring's afternoon dance came, Marcus Orford dressed himself with more care than usual, and, in company with several others of the officers of the Black Horse, set off for that lady's house in the regimental break. Urquhart up to the last moment left it uncertain whether he would go or not.

"Am I going to Lady Mainwaring's afternoon dance or not?" he repeated after Orford. "No, I don't think I am. Afternoon dances are altogether out of my line. I don't want to dance with anybody, and I don't suppose anybody wants to dance with me. Why should they?"

"Because you're one of the best waltzers in England, and because you're commanding officer of the Black Horse," Orford answered. ·

" Pretty reasons those; can't you give me any more likely ones?" Urquhart inquired derisively.

Orford burst out laughing.

" Yes; to be sure I can. First, because you are very well off; secondly, because you are just a nice suitable age to have come to the end of your wild oats and be thinking of settling down to the cultivation of a respectable matrimonial harvest; thirdly, or rather, in addition to the two reasons I gave you first—fifthly—fifthly, because you are not what most people would consider too hideous to be interesting; and sixth and lastly, and most strong and cogent reason of all, because, from some absurd mistake or other, a sort of idea has got afloat that you are by way of being a woman-hater."

" Oh, they always say that of a man who isn't particularly keen about getting married," Urquhart returned slightingly.

" Of course they do; it adds to the general interest of the creature," Orford laughed. " Well, are you going ? "

" I don't think so. I don't feel up to dancing to-day. I've never got over that wrench of my knee."

" But you can talk; there'll be heaps of people to talk to," Orford persisted.

" Will there ? Anybody worth talking to ? "

" There'll be Mrs Traff."

Urquhart gave a short, amused laugh.

" Ye gods! what an inducement to set out for

a man's delectation. 'Pon my word, Marcus,
your idea of 'a dainty dish, to set before the
king' is really too refreshing. Mrs Traff!
She'll be asking me to get her a tom-cat or
a kangaroo next. No; I've got the colley
pup, and I've done the civil at No. 7 twice.
For mercy's sake let me keep out of the
old girl's clutches as long as possible."

"Well, I wish you'd go," Orford persisted,
and turning over the little trifling knick-
knacks, with which the chimney-shelf was
ornamented, with such a disconsolate air that
Urquhart's heart was quite touched with
pity. In his way Colonel Urquhart was
more attached to him than to any other
officer in his regiment, and when alone the
two invariably relapsed into the familiar
tone of the old days when they had been
subalterns together.

"Do you *want* me to go?" he asked, with
a change of tone. "Have you any particular
reason for wishing me to go?"

"Well, I want to go myself, and—and—
that Mrs Traff's eyes go spying all over the
place, you know; but if *you* were there
she'd have no time to be looking after me.
She—she—oh! hang it all, Urquhart, you
know what I mean. She may be all very
well, but she will insist on making things
what she calls a little pleasant for me, and
she makes a great parade of it, and then she

plants that Julia on me, and, hang it, I can-*not* stand it, and that's all about it."

Urquhart laid back in his chair, and laughed long and loudly.

" The widow Traff' is too much for you, eh ? " he exclaimed. " Well, we'll see what I can do for you in the protection line. Come in ! " he added, in reply to a knock upon the panel of the door. " Oh ! is that you, Durrant ? " turning his head as the orderly officer for the day entered.

Marcus Orford rose to go.

" Then shall I count upon you, Colonel ? " he added.

" Yes, Orford, certainly," was the reply, and then Orford went away, feeling that without doubt Urquhart was a real good fellow at bottom, and that it was simply a thousand pities that he had ever been compelled by circumstances, of which seniority was of course the chief one, to take to the heavy father style of business, which was the fashion in which Orford invariably spoke and thought of the enviable and delectable position of an officer in command of a regiment.

And so it came about that the hour of four that afternoon saw the Colonel and Orford entering Lady Mainwaring's drawing-room together.

" So delighted to see you," said that lady graciously ; then some other people came, and with a bow the two officers safely passed the Rubicon, and found themselves within the room with no fear of immediate introduction before them.

However, in less than a moment they had fallen a prey to Mrs Traff, who had ensconced herself in a position practically commanding the door, and having brought a pair of powerful double glasses to bear upon that point had made escape impossible.

"*So* pleased. What a lovely change in the weather," she gushed out. "Oh! *how* do you do, Captain Orford? I have not seen you for ages. Julia, my dear, do you not see Captain Orford? Colonel Urquhart, the dear colley is quite *too* amusing. You must come and see him, he is getting such a big fellow."

"I hope he behaves himself properly," said Colonel Urquhart politely.

"Oh! *per*-fectly," then she broke off suddenly and levelled her glasses at the door. "Ow—de—ah!" Mrs Traff always overdid her accent when she wanted to be more extensive than ordinary. "Who ev-ah can *these* people be?".

She knew perfectly well who *these* people were, but that was beside the question. *These* people, as it happened, were Mrs Hugh Antrobus and the fair Polly. Mrs Hugh came in beaming like a harvest moon, and subsided in a fat mass on the sofa by Mrs Traff. Mrs Traff made room for her with an air which savoured very much of drawing her skirts away from touch with a contagious disease or a bad character.

Polly looked simply lovely. And two very young officers asked to be introduced to her immediately.

"Such a mistake," observed Mrs Traff' in a loud murmur to her neighbour, Mrs Morning-ton-Brown, "of Lady Mainwaring to ask such people. Ow—yes, quite a mistake. I nev-ah do it. It always seems odd to me that in Blankhampton," she added aloud—I mean by that very much aloud, "that there are so many people one does not know. Juli-ah! Juli-ah, my de-ah, have you asked *Cap*-tain Orford about the theatricals?"

"What is that?" Orford asked.

He would at any time rather talk to Mrs Traff' than Juli-ah, not that she was the most pleasant, but then she was the least compromising.

"Ow! We are getting up some amateuah theatricals in aid of dear Miss Courtenay's Maternity House."

"Oh! really—er—by-the-bye, Mrs Traff-ord," remembering just in time to add the last syl-lable to the good lady's name, "er—what *is* a Maternity House?"

Mrs Traff' made haste to answer, for Colonel Urquhart was looking grimly amused, and she had an idea he was laughing at her.

"It is a home for poor moth-ahs, Mr Orford. Ow—I beg your pardon, *Cap*-tain Orford. I shall nev-ah remember to address you in the new fashion," alluding to Orford's having recently obtained his troop.

Orford thought, if the truth be told, that her acquaintance with him being a thing of yesterday, it was surprising that she found any difficulty at all in the matter.

"Oh! I see," he went on. "And what are the theatricals?"

"They are to be in the theatre—two grand nights. One under the patronage of the Lord-Lieutenant, the High Sheriff, and the Judges of the Assize; the other by General Gardner and the officers of the garrison, and I have promised to try to persuade Colonel Urquhart," with quite a little coquettish air, and an uplifting, not of her eyes—Mrs Traff's eyes were not her strong point—but of her sharp little nose, in a way which made Urquhart lift his eyebrows a shade, and Orford feel as if his clothes had suddenly got too tight for him, and he was threatened with a fit of apoplexy, " to bespeak a third night — just Colonel Urquhart and the officers of the Black Horse."

"Oh! yes," Orford broke in, without giving his chief time to answer. "And are you going to act, Mrs Trafford."

"Ow, no, Captain Orford; I shall help a good deal. My girls are going to act—at least, Laura will act, and Juli-ah is going to sing between the parts."

"That will be very charming," said Orford,
with a bow to Miss Julia. "And what is your
niece going to do? Has she any part?"

"Ow, now;" at the mention of her niece, Mrs
Traff's accent got even more affected; "she has
no talent at all in that way. My niece is not a
soci-aty girl at all."

"Thank God!" muttered Orford in Urquhart's
ear, to the enlightenment of that gentleman's
mind, and very much to the gratification of his
curiosity. "Indeed. Is she here to-day?"

"No, not to-day," very sweetly, so sweetly
that he knew instantly she had not been allowed to come. "She is not very well."

It was astonishing how soon after this Marcus Orford contrived to sheer off, but not
before he had witnessed as pretty a bit of
comedy as he ever remembered to have seen
in all his life, for just as Lord Charterhouse—
one of the last-joined subalterns of the regiment
—went off in triumph with the fair Polly to
the room where there was dancing, Lady Mainwaring came up to the sofa on which the
proud and benignant Mrs Hugh was sitting
beside the eminently exclusive and disgusted
Mrs Traff.

"Captain Orford, pray let me find you a
partner," she said. "Not just yet? Oh, well.
if you have had a hard day's work I must let
you off. Dear Mrs Trafford, I particularly want
to introduce Mrs Antrobus to you. I am quite

sure you will like each other immensely," and
then her ladyship sailed off to speak to another
guest.

Mrs Traff' was perfectly furious; yet, although
common politeness had not compelled Lady
Mainwaring to inquire whether the introduction would be acceptable or not, that same in-
valuable bar to all manner of disagreeable
scenes prevented her from receiving it in any
but the ordinary course.

Mrs Hugh beamed with satisfaction, for to
her the introduction to Mrs Traff' was as great
a thing as it would be for Mrs Traff' to be
introduced to the Mauleverers, with the addi-
tional information to those stiff-necked and
haughty spinsters that they would be quite
sure to like her immensely.

And poor Mrs Hugh, bent upon improving
the occasion, was quite unconscious of the disgust which filled Mrs Traff's soul, and showed
itself in the way she threw her head back and
half closed her eyes, as if there was a very
strong blaze of sunlight upon her, and she was
not very sure whether Mrs Hugh was one yard
away from her or ten.

And her drawling, mincing, muttering became
so pronounced that Urquhart began to have
grave doubts whether she might not find herself
severely biting her own tongue.

Nor could she very well get away from this
objectionable new acquaintance, who would in-

sist on being very friendly and confidential with her, for when Lady Mainwaring had introduced the two good ladies, she had at the same time introduced Colonel Urquhart to the fair Polly's mamma; and Colonel Urquhart having undertaken to keep Mrs Traff's attention off Orford's doings, found the task quite as pleasant in Mrs Hugh's very graphic and amusing conversation · about the ABBOT-ABBOTS of ABBOTSWELL, and other such cherished topics of hers as he would have done in any one else's, and, if the truth be told, a very great deal more pleasant than if he had been condemned to what was practically a *tête-à-tête* with Mrs Traff', and compelled to stand his ground under the awful fire of her elderly coquetries.

Meantime Orford had gone the round of the company and found himself near the door, just as Lester Brookes arrived.

"Hollo, Orford, looking after the Colonel, eh?" he laughed, as a greeting.

"Yes."

"Why, there they are in full swing. God bless me, I never would have believed that the Colonel was capable of it, if I hadn't seen it with my own eyes. My word, but Mrs Traff' as an *ingenue* is a sight worth seeing. Ye gods, how she is going it. Who's the stout old par-tay on the other side?"

"Can't say, I'm sure—got a very pretty daughter," Orford answered.

"Really. By-the-bye, I met Miss Trafford just now."

"Where ? " eagerly.

"Just going into the Winter Gardens."

"Ah !—I say, there's that pretty girl, dancing with Charterhouse."

"I'll go and get introduced," returned Brookes, with an alacrity which he usually showed in running after a pretty face.

And as Brookes turned to go across the room Marcus Orford slipped out into the hall, found his hat with some little difficulty, and closing the door very softly behind him—bolted !

SIDELIGHT.

MADGE TRAFFORD.

ONCE—I will tell it in a whisper, because she herself never did even that much—Madge Trafford was coming back to her father's house in Brompton from a shopping expedition.

It was near the time of Christmas. The shop windows were gay with tempting and pretty trifles, and mirth and festivity were the order of the day. But, alas! in the City of the World you can never get far away from misery of the worst kind, and Madge, as she turned out of the main road towards her home, came upon a wretched woman carrying a baby at her bare and starved looking breast, while three tiny dots tugged and dragged at the skirts of her clothing. She was trying to sing, and succeeding only in making the winter dusk hideous. As Madge reached her the doleful wail came to an end and she held forth a skinny, supplicating hand.

"Kind lady, kind lady," she said, in pleading tones.

Madge opened her purse—but it was empty, for she had spent all.

"I have spent all my money, I can't give you anything," she said ruefully; "but—here, I'll try what I can do for you," and forthwith she stepped off the pavement on to the frost-bound road and raised her voice to the keen evening air. It trembled slightly at first, but gained strength as she sang, not to man but to God Himself in Heaven above:—

> "Oh! cruel lamps of London,
>   If tears your lights could drown,
>   Your victims' eyes would weep them,
>   Oh! lights of London town."

And oh! how happy that wretched woman went to her poor home that night.

Madge kept silence; but a little bird told me.

CHAPTER VII.

UNDER THE MULBERRY TREE.

AS he turned out of the Close into the High Street, he shook himself into his usual gait, and set off for the Winter Gardens as fast as his long legs and his smart feet could carry him. But when he reached them, he sauntered in as if he had come there quite by accident, and when he came upon Miss Madge Trafford, sitting on a bench under a mulberry tree, with a parasol and a book, the intensity of his surprise was really beyond everything.

Now, Miss Trafford was honestly surprised to see him there. For days past, the subject of her cousin Julia's new dress for Lady Mainwaring's afternoon dance had been under discussion, she having the credit from her mother of having made "quite great friends with *Captain Orford*," and being specially charged with the duty of trying to make Blankhampton a little pleasant to him! And then to see the object of this solicitude sauntering about the Winter Gardens as if he were a poor, lonely, desolate thing, snubbed by everybody, and not knowing a soul in the world who would say a single kind word to him—why, it certainly was rather astonishing.

"Why are you not at the dance?" she asked, as he took her hand.

"The dance?" blankly. "Lady Mainwaring's afternoon dance? Oh, yes. I did just look in, but I don't know that dancing is much in my line."

If only the officers of the Black Horse could but have heard this new idea! For it was new; he being quite the show man of the regiment for that sort of thing.

"Really? I should have thought you were rather good at it. I was so surprised to see you."

"I might say the same—only, of course, I saw you were not at Lady Mainwaring's. How is it you did not go? Are you not well?"

"Oh, perfectly, thanks;" and, indeed, she looked the very picture of blooming health. "No; the truth is, I don't very often go to that sort of entertainment. You see, it would be rather a tax on my aunt having always to take three girls about with her, and I don't really care anything about it. My cousins, on the contrary, are fond of all kinds of society."

"And you don't care much about it?"

"Not for Blankhampton society," smiling.

"Neither do I," Orford chimed in heartily.
He would have agreed with anything that she
said, but since he really agreed with this remark
with all his heart and soul, he uttered the rejoinder with a vigorous cordiality such as made
Madge Trafford fancy her cousin Julia had not
succeeded very well in her philanthropic efforts
in his direction.

"You see, I was brought up in London," she
told him. "My father was an artist, and knew
a good many people. And he has not been dead
very long—only three years—so that really I
feel quite like a fish out of water. Everything
is so different in a place like Blankhampton.
People think so much of what we used to think
nothing at all."

"How you must have hated it."

"I did, just at first. But I am used to it now,
and perhaps some day I shall go back again.
Who knows?"

"Ah, who knows, indeed? Er—may I sit
down? Do you mind?"

"Not at all," making room for him on the
bench beside her.

Marcus Orford sat down with a blessed feeling
of contentment. After all, the world was very
good to live in, particularly when things happened in the kaleidoscope of life to fall into the
exact pattern which suited his fancy or conveni-

ence.   He had been so bitterly disappointed
when he did not find her at the dance, so disgusted that he had inveigled the Colonel into
going, so sorry to hear that *she* was not well.

And then, when Lester Brookes put his good-
tempered handsome face in at the door, and told
that he had seen her go into the Winter Gardens,
why, hope began to spring up within his breast,
a tiny flower dreading the return of the chill
breath of disappointment, yet by the time he
reached the mulberry tree, grown strong and
high, until it rivalled the mustard seed of the
Scriptures for speed and highness.

And almost the first thing she said, was that
she was perfectly well, and she looked it.

" So the old cat told me a lie," said Marcus
Orford to himself " I shall have to take care
what I am after with her.   I thought she hadn't
that face for nothing."

" What are these theatricals that are coming
off ? " he asked, shaking himself free of his
thoughts.

Madge Trafford laughed outright.

" They are the very greatest joke in the world.
It is a club, at least a dramatic society, which
prides itself on being framed on the model of
the Busy Bees.   They have been giving enter-
tainments ever since I was here, and quarrel
frightfully.   Oh, it is the very greatest joke in
the world—to anyone with a sense of humour.
They all want to be leading ladies, you know,

and to take quite girls' parts. Now, last winter
we had 'Meg's Diversion' and 'Ici on Parle
Français,' and really the whole affair was an
awful joke. *That* was in aid of the restoration
of the nave, and they got the Dean to act as
president. We had most of the committee meet-
ings at our house—my aunt is great at organi-
sation you know—so I heard all the fun. Our
leading lady of all—they are all leading ladies,
you know, but this one, Mrs de Carteret, stands
first and foremost, because she played a good
deal in India and the Bermudas; in fact, *there*
she was considered infinitely superiòr to Mrs
Bancroft for high comedy, and a great deal more
fetching than Mrs Kendal in pathetic parts,
while she was acknowledged by *every*body,"
with an expansive gesture, "to be beyond com-
parison with any other actress on the English
stage."

"Dear me, is she going to act this time?" Orford exclaimed.

"This time? She *al*-ways acts! She will
take the principal part in the piece, and the best
one in the farce. She gets all the 'fat' invariably. I told her so once, and she said I was so
coarse I really made her feel quite ill."

"Poor soul!"

"When you see her play a pathetic part you
will indeed say 'Poor soul!' To hear her weep-
ing is something too awful! But the performance
is not the cream of her efforts; the rehearsals are

so immensely funny that when the great night comes, and order and decorum reign, it all seems very, very flat after the bickering and backbiting of the rehearsals. First she lays down a rule—to which everyone else must adhere under pain of instant death or something nearly as awful—that everything is to be done as regularly and as punctually as if they were in a professional company receiving regular treasury. The rehearsals are to be under the sole direction of the stage-manager; no one else is to say a single word or give a single direction except him. His word is to be law.

"Then, when everybody has cordially agreed thereto, the rehearsals begin. Mrs de Carteret sits book in hand at one of the wings.

"'That's not right,' she calls out, at the first slip. 'Look here! You must do so and so. You don't mind my telling you, do you? You see, of course, I am thoroughly *au fait* of *all* these little things.'

"But when the time comes for Mrs de Carteret to begin she is found to be no more letter-perfect than any one else. 'Of course that will be all right on the night,' she says loftily. 'No one ever does those little things in rehearsal;' and this is the sort of thing that the others don't seem to see, when they are drilled and marshalled and ordered here and there, as if they were so many novices at fifteen shillings a week in a company doing the provinces.

"The last performances they gave were even more prolific of envy, hatred, and all uncharitableness than usual. They were going to do 'Married Life'; however, that had to be thrown up, because there were too many good parts in it—they were too equal in 'fat.' It was quite impossible for Mrs de Carteret to do Mrs Younghusband, Mrs Dove, Mrs Dismal, Mrs Coddle, *and* Mrs Lynx. That is to say, it was impossible for her to play them all. If it had been possible, she would have done so. She cast herself at once for Mrs Younghusband, though she is getting on for forty, and has not much further to go before she gets there. Perhaps she is rather good-looking, and some people think she has a good figure. Still, she takes all the young girls' parts, although there are several young girls of very promising talent in the club.

"So 'Married Life' was thrown up, and 'War to the Knife' was chosen instead, Mrs de Carteret casting herself for the part of the lively young widow. With an immense amount of trouble and wrangling the cast was completed; this one was too tall, that too old, they wanted a *young* person for this, and a *slim* one for the other. But eventually 'War to the Knife' was thrown up, because Mrs Donnithorne, the wife of the senior major in the last regiment, finding by some side wind that she, though a good ten years younger than Mrs de Carteret, was considered by that lady of too elderly appearance to play the part of Mrs Harcourt, threw that part up, and took instead that of the middle-aged servant which was going begging. With most people this would have been concession enough, but our leading lady wasn't satisfied. She wanted Mrs Donnithorne out of the cast altogether, so took bitter offence because that lady said one day with a laugh, when she forgot her servant's part for a moment, 'Dear me, I keep forgetting that I'm not a lady now.'"

"But what was there to take offence at in that?" asked Orford, who was deeply interested in this choice, and, to him, new dish of garrison gossip.

"Oh! well, you see, Mrs de Carteret had by her own wish taken the part of Betsy Baker for the farce. They do say she was once a servant herself, and that she took Mrs Donnithorne's remark as personal. Anyway, there was an awful row, and a special meeting in my aunt's drawing-room, with the Dean in the chair. My aunt was comfortably out of it, and Laura was not much involved, so we thoroughly enjoyed ourselves, all of us. And the result was that all the people belonging to the Yellow Horse withdrew the light of their countenances, and Mrs de Carteret had the pleasure of playing a powder and patches part, in which she was the only lady of the piece. Just what suited her."

"Is she the D. A. A. G.'s wife?"

"Yes. He is a very pompous sort of person."

"Oh! I know him—little fat man, with a red face."

"Yes, that is the man. We found out afterwards though, that Mrs Donnithorne's real offence was not so much in what she ostensibly offended, but because, with a view of making things pleasant all round, she resigned the part of Mrs Harcourt in favour of Mrs Philip Messant, of the Blankshire Regiment. She, it seems, was great at theatricals, and her husband happening to hear of the complaint made of Mrs Donnithorne's appearance, said that his wife was coming the following week, and he was sure she would act if they needed another.

"We heard afterwards that Mrs de Carteret asked Lord Alfred Pierrepoint if he knew Mrs Messant? Oh! he did. What was she like?

"Lord Alfred said he had only seen the lady once, but had danced with her; that she was tall and slim, rather distinguished-looking, but very plain.

"Under these circumstances Mrs Messant's services were gladly accepted; and then she appeared at rehearsal, word-perfect, with a good knowledge of acting, but was, instead of being what Lord Alfred described her,—a wee, tiny, dainty little beauty. It was too much for Mrs de Carteret, and that was the real reason 'War to the Knife' came to grief."

"Pierrepoint had mistaken her?"

"Yes, for her sister. One of the Yellow Horse officers wrote a sort of little fable about it and had it printed. Oh! how funny. I have my pocket-book here. I pasted it into it lest I should lose it. Here it is."

SIDELIGHT.

MRS DE CARTERET.

SOME people said she was a perfect skeleton. They might have said worse — for if she was a perfect skeleton, at the same time her skeleton was perfect. She was thin, true, but she was an exquisite shape, and with a couple of stones more flesh upon her bones would have been a magnificent woman.

And she was handsome too, though her nose was rather too long, and a shade too prominent. She sang—oh, my! *how* she did sing, songs of the most pronounced and florid type, generally Italian—"*Una voce*" for instance— she used to say Italian brought the voice out, a remark which generally made her hearers wish she would stick to English. Then besides her singing, she acted! She acted anything and everything, from the most sombre tragedy to burlesque! She *liked* high comedy, very high. On one occasion she got up two grand performances of a highly popular piece, casting herself for one of Mrs Bernard Beere's most successful parts. She took great pains to ensure big houses, infinite care to procure the best amateurs (men) to be found in the whole of the Service; she had a dozen working rehearsals, and four full-dress ones—*àpropos* of dresses, she had three expensive costumes made for herself out of the proceeds, which swallowed up most of the money, to the detriment of the charity for which the affair was brought about—and then? Well, when the great night came a brilliant audience assembled to witness a performance by several clever soldiers and one stick: the stick was Mrs de Carteret.

CHAPTER VIII.

"THE DAISY IN THE PATCH OF TURF!"

HE handed her pocket-book to him as she spoke, and Orford read,—

"THE DAISY IN THE PATCH OF TURF!

"Once upon a time there was a patch of turf which bore blades of grass of different sorts. Some were tall, others were short, some were stiff, others were limp; some were fresh, others were faded; some were broad, and others were narrow. But they were all alike in one respect; they were all blades of grass.

"Well, in the midst of the patch there grew a daisy, and she was the centre of attraction, though she had never been a very fine specimen of a daisy, and her light was the light of other days. Still, she was a daisy; she was the one flower among all those blades of grass, so that

even the youngest and freshest and greenest of
them was infinitely inferior to her.

"Other flowers would willingly have shed the
light and beauty of their bloom over the litte patch
of turf. A yellow marigold offered herself, but
the daisy flouted her. 'Who knows this marigold?' said she to the blades of grass. '*I* never
heard of her. If we give her leave to grow in
the patch of grass, she will want to stand in the
middle where *I* am.' So the marigold was sent
about her business."

"Who was the marigold?" Orford asked.

"One of the surgeon's wives, who had been
in the profession," she answered. "The buttercup was another officer's wife who had been an
actress."

So Orford read on.

"Then a dainty young buttercup offered her
services.

"'Painted thing,' cried the daisy. 'Who
wants her yellow tints? There is quite enough
yellow in my eye to light up the whole patch.'
So the buttercup had to follow the marigold.
And the daisy continued to grow in the middle
of the patch of turf until by-and-by she came
to imagine herself to be no longer a daisy, but
the very rarest of hot-house blooms.

"'See how I look,' she cried to the blades of
grass. 'Ah! how dull, how ungainly you all
are. You are such common things.'

"So she showed this one how to stand, that

one how to balance gracefully against the wind,
a third how to sway to and fro. But when a
lark came and rested on the patch for a moment
she cried, 'Away, away; we want no singing-
birds here. You are too coarse and big and
old for us—'"

" Who was the lark ?" Orford inquired.

" Mrs Donnithorne."

" Oh ! I see," reading on.

" And to the linnet, 'Away with you, away
with you. If you come singing here, *I* shall
bloom no longer.'

"And after that she went on educating the
blades of grass—how to sit, how to stand, how
to flutter and sway in the breeze and, most of
all, how to do homage to her.

" But by-and-by the blades of grass began to
grow weary of so much homage and of so much
education. 'She is only a daisy after all,' they
said. 'She does not stand so very well herself
that she need always be so ready to show us;
she does not flutter or sway in the breeze half
so gracefully as some of us; and, after all, she
is not an orchid, nor a camellia, nor a spray of
stephanotis, no, nor even a peony. She is only
a daisy.'

"And by-and-by the patch began to look
rather bare, particularly in one place, that where
the lark, who was too big and plump and *old*
would have stood if the daisy had let her.
Therefore one of the blades of grass suggested

that, if the daisy would allow it, he would persuade his wife to come and grow there.

"'What is she like?' asked someone in the
daisy's hearing.

"'Oh,' answered another, 'she is very tall and
thin, even ungainly—but she is not common.'

"So she was allowed to come. But lo! and
behold, when she came, not a mere ordinary
blade of grass, but a fair, fresh, sweet lily of
the valley, who took her place beside the daisy,
who was *only* a daisy, after all.

"'Dig the patch up,' cried the daisy to the
garden-spade, 'the blades of grass will not own
that I am the fairest flower in the world—let
them perish!'

"So the poor blades of grass got the credit,
but it was without doubt the lily of the valley
that did the mischief."

"Finest thing I ever read," Orford cried;
"what a clever fellow he must have been to
think of all that—it was the lily of the valley
that did the mischief. Ah, lilies of the valley
generally do no end of mischief, particularly
when their lot is cast among common daisies
which think themselves orchids or tuberoses."

His tone was so marked and so significant
that Madge Trafford felt herself suddenly called
back to the realities of life; to the fact that the
afternoon was fast waning, and that she was
sitting under a mulberry tree with the man for
whose delectation her cousin Julia had arrayed

herself, like Solomon in all his glory, in a new gown, and had set forth like a giant refreshed with wine to do battle and great slaughter at Lady Mainwaring's dance.

And, behold, here was the man who had waited not for the fray, but had turned aside from the battle without so much as a dint in his cuirass, or the least sign of a scratch on his armour. Depend upon it, they—that is, her aunt and cousins—would not go home in the very best of tempers, the very idea of which was enough to make her draw out her watch and consult it eagerly.

"A quarter to seven; what an age we have been here! I had no idea it was so late," she cried. "I must go. Good-bye—no, don't come with me; better not, as you shirked the dance. It would not look very well if anyone told Lady Mainwaring."

"I will go to the gate, if you will let me—please do," he pleaded; and as she did not gainsay him, he walked beside her to the gates. But there she parted from him and sent him back.

"A lot of smart people are coming down the street," she said, peering through the bushes. "You go back, it is no use offending Lady Mainwaring for nothing; after she has been so kind as to make a party for you. You must say when you see her that the heat of the room was too much for you."

"So it was."

"Yes; I daresay. Good-bye."

She gave him a last little nod and went at a moderate pace up the street, turning the corner into St Eve's and reaching the door of No. 7 just as her aunt and the two girls reached it from the opposite direction.

"How very tiresome you are, Madge!" exclaimed Mrs Traff' crossly. "Why need you have gone out this afternoon, and in any case have been coming home just at this time?"

"I did not know there was any reason why I should not, Aunt Marion," returned the girl mildly.

"You make it so difficult for me," said Mrs Traff' fretfully. "Captain Orford asked for you, and I was obliged to make some excuse for your not being there, and I said you were not very well. It makes it so very difficult, when the first person I see when I get outside the house is you, looking the very picture of aggressive health."

Quickly as lightning the thought flashed into Madge Trafford's mind that she had better say nothing of her having seen the man to whom and for whom this untruth had been told.

"But it does not altogether matter," Mrs Traff' went on, in weary accents, "for Captain Orford did not stay half-an-hour."

"Why; wasn't he well?" Madge asked.

"He *looked* all right—I think it is Lady Mainwaring's fault. She will persist in mixing her people so incongruously. Imagine, of all

people in Blankhampton, she had that Mrs
Antrobus and her daughter there. And Lord
Charterhouse made quite a parade of his attention to the girl, and Lady Mainwaring positively
introduced the mother to ME."

"Mrs Antrobus? The stout old lady?"
Madge asked.

"Yes—to *me*—and without giving me the
faintest chance of declining it; said she knew
we should like each other immensely," answered
Mrs Traff', in accents of unutterable disgust. " I
was as stiff and distant as possible, but it was
no use. She had the impertinence to tell me
she intends to call upon me. Of course, Captain
Orford disappeared at once, and *I* never saw
him after."

"I saw him steal out of the hall door," said
Laura Traff', laughing; "and it was not very
long before the Colonel went after him."

"Oh, that woman was cause enough to
frighten any men away," sighed Mrs Traff',
with the air of a hawk which has been robbed
of its prey.

Oh, Mrs Traff', Mrs Traff', if you had only
known that to find the cause of Urquhart's and
Orford's defection you need not, indeed, have
looked so far a-field as Mrs Hugh, with her fat
smile and her self-complaisance! In fact, that
you might have looked so nearly at home as at
the original and the second editions of a pert
little nose of that class which poets call "tip-

tilted," and of a high-pitched, squeaky voice with a crack in it. If you had only known that !

There is a verse of poetry which says, and says wisely :—

> " Oh, wad some power the giftie gie us,
> Tae see ourselves as ithers see us,
> It wad frae mony a blunder free us,
>   And foolish notion ! "

But though that would have been very good for you, it would have been very bad for those who were watching the wonderful game of " sassiety " in Blankhampton.

SIDELIGHT.

MRS TRAFF'.

UNDOUBTEDLY she was a very clever little woman. For instance, in the game of society there is a good deal to be made out of a reputation for being musical, and Mrs Traff', on the strength of Julia's good voice and Laura's slender little pipe, and her own capability of playing the accompaniment to a song at a pinch — very much at a pinch—certainly took her change out of the money she had expended in music and singing masters. And as there is much to be made out of music, so is there more to be made out of charity—and Mrs Traff' made it. She went in for being very charitable, and like a clever little woman, she managed to accomplish the not very easy feat of being charitable out of other people's pockets. There is nothing so easy in this life as to bear other folk's troubles, or to bury other folk's bairns, but it is really a very difficult thing to give away other folk's money. But *she* did it—regularly.

"Oh! dear, dear, how ill your poor little girl looks," she cried to a poor dressmaker one day. "I must see what *I* can do for her!"

So she begged a few soup tickets of one; invalid-kitchen tickets of another; a frock of a third; a hat of a fourth; boots of a fifth, and a convalescent home ticket of a sixth; and then she gathered a few shillings at one of her afternoons after the Parish, and sent the sick child off to win health and strength in a month at the seaside. It cost a good deal of trouble, but not a penny of money, and every one said what a *kind* heart she had, and how *good* she was to the poor.

Clever little Mrs Traff'!

CHAPTER IX.

A GRIM JOKE.

WO days after this Mrs Traff' sent out invitations for a dinner - party, and when Marcus Orford received his, which was by the afternoon post, he put on his hat and went straight away in search of the Colonel. He found him in his own sitting-room.

"I say, Urquhart," he began, as he opened the door.

The Colonel looked up from his book, which, by the way, was a novel by a fashionable authoress.

"What is it?" he asked: he was very strongly attached to Orford, and the feeling had deepened with the flight of years. "Anything the matter?"

"Oh, no; but I say, have you got an invitation to dine at Mrs Traff's? Oh, I see you have.

H-m; I'll tell you what, Urquhart, that old woman means doing for you."

"Doing for me! How?"

"Marrying you, of course."

"Oh, marrying me," repeated Colonel Urquhart, with no little amusement: then some devil, some stray vestige of the old Adam which had possessed him in the days when he was only a subaltern or a junior among the captains, rose up within him and took possession of him. "Well, on the whole," he said deliberately, "she might do worse."

Orford's astonishment was so great that his jaw dropped until he looked like a cod-fish in the last agonies, instead of a handsome young man of more than ordinary attractiveness. He was so astonished that he relapsed at once into the formal mode of address which he employed when others were present.

"Oh, well, of course, Colonel, if that's it, I'm awfully sorry I said anything," he stammered. "I didn't know. I hadn't the least idea of it." And then he bolted out of the room as if he was a fox with a pack of hounds after him.

As Colonel Urquhart heard Orford's footsteps die away in the hall, and then saw him pass the window on his way back to the mess-rooms for his own quarters, he lay back in his big chair and simply laughed till he cried, till the tears actually streamed down his cheeks, and for a few minutes he could not have spoken to save his soul alive.

And then he struggled up and sat weakly chuckling, until the fits of laughter came on once more, and convulsed him worse than before.

" Good heavens ! what a face he put on," he cried to himself. " If I live to be a thousand I shall never forget it. Fancy Marcus taken in like that. What a joke ! "

Yes, it certainly was a joke. But all the same, Marcus Orford had gone straight into the ante-room, where the majority of the officers of the regiment were gathered with several officers of other regiments quartered in the garrison, and blurted out the news at once as *a positive fact.*

" I say, you fellows," he gasped, rather than spoke, " have you heard the news ? "

" No : what news ? " asked Brookes.

" About what ? " demanded Dayrell, seeing from Orford's face that something out of the common had taken place.

" About the Colonel : he's going to marry Mrs Traff "."

" *What !* " cried Dayrell.

" He's engaged to her ; told me so himself just now. By George ! he's *gone* on her too ; says she might do worse—*that she might do worse !* Only think of it. Do you realise it ? "

"Not a bit," returned Dayrell promptly. "I don't believe a word of it."

"Neither do I," said Sir Anthony Staunton.

"It's true. Urquhart was as grave as a judge about it," Orford persisted.

"Imagine Mrs Traff' as a blushing bride," observed Eden, with feeling.

"Imagine the poor old regiment with her in command," groaned Orford—then added, with conviction, "I shall leave."

"Oh, no, you won't, my dear boy," laughed Brookes. "You'll be best man, take my word for it."

"Best man!—the poor beggar's second, you mean," Orford rejoined sharply. "If it had been anybody else I shouldn't have been surprised — widows are so insinuating, and Mrs Traff's got a little way with her that's very taking at times; but Urquhart—Urquhart of *all* men on the face of God's earth. I can*not* realise it! Now, if it had been you, Colonel Coles, I shouldn't have been surprised a bit."

"But I should," returned the gossip, with emphasis. "I should be so surprised that I shouldn't know myself when I looked in the glass of a morning to shave."

"Old Coles 'll say ta-ta in a minute," muttered Dayrell to Lester Brookes, who was standing beside him.

"What makes you think so?"

"Old gossip—he'll rush off to his quarters and

get dressed, and go down town and call on every
blessed house he knows. Gad, he don't often
get such a tit-bit to retail over the afternoon
teas.   I wonder where he'll go first?   Mrs
Traff's, I shouldn't wonder.   Ah ! there he goes
—told you so."

"Yes, must go," Coles was saying.   "Got some
business to do in town—by-by."

Dayrell burst out laughing as the door closed
behind him.

"Happy old soul !" he exclaimed. "He is just
like a dog with an extra choice bone. He'll be
off at once.   By-the-bye, I owe Mrs Traff a call ;
I think I'll go down this afternoon ; it would be
rather a joke to hear old Coles congratulate her."

"I'll go with you," said Brookes.   "But I say,
Dayrell, do you think it's true ?"

"Not at all unlikely.   Urquhart has always
been a little difficult about women ; it seems
queer, certainly, but in marriages the unforeseen
always seems to happen."

The old gossip was already off to his quarters
in the town, with a view to changing his uniform
for plain clothes, and as soon as this was accomplished, he set off for the house of the widow Traff
without delay.   He found that little lady very
busily engaged in sending out notices of the
next rehearsal, she being secretary to the Blankhampton Amateur Theatrical Club.

"Oh, Colonel Coles, how you do ?" she cried,
beaming at him through her half-closed eyelids.

"*Quite* well, thanks; er—er— I understand I am to congratulate you, Mrs Trafford," he answered, plunging at once into the business of the visit.

"That is very good of you; thanks, very many." And then, just as she was about to ask the cause of his congratulations, the door opened, and the maid ushered in Captain Dayrell and Mr Brookes.

Mrs Traff' beamed! For she loved a lord as dearly as her hopes of heaven, and Dayrell, being the son of a nobleman, was a thrice welcome guest.

"I hope you are quite well, Mrs Trafford," said Lester Brookes, with his soldier's air of modesty.

"Oh! quite well, thanks. Is not this weather delightful?"

"Charming," said Dayrell; then looked at the old gossip and raised his eyebrows a shade, as if to say, "Have you asked her?"

The gossip nodded in reply, and Dayrell's eyebrows asked another question, "Is it true?"

And the gossip, Mrs Traff' having accepted his congratulations, as he thought, whereas in truth the little woman was all in the dark and could not imagine what he meant, again nodded in answer.

Dayrell's eyebrows went up a good deal more than a shade at that, but as his chief had not as yet announced the engagement formally, he, of

course, had to be content with taking his information at second hand from Colonel Coles, instead of congratulating the lady himself. And
how heartily did he curse himself for not having
been ten minutes earlier, and so been present
when the gossip approached the subject.

" I am so sorry my daughters are not at home,"
said Mrs Traff,' as she began to dispense the tea
which the neat maid had brought, and she said
it, mother-like, with feeling. " What ? You
came to see me ? Oh! Mr Brookes, that is a
very pretty speech to make to an old woman."

" Not very *old*," said Dayrell politely.

" Not very *young*," rejoined Mrs Traff', with a
laugh.

It was surprising how interesting she had become all at once. The three men watched her
every movement with lynx eyes, and, if the
truth be told, one thought, one question upper-
most in each of their minds, and the question
was: "What the devil *can* Urquhart be thinking
of ?" for Mrs Traff' was, in truth, a very un-
attractive little person, in spite of a remark
which Orford had made less than an hour before,
to the effect that widows were so insinuating,
and that Mrs Traff' had a very taking way with
her at times. And before many minutes had
passed by, the neat maid appeared once more in
advance of two other gentlemen, both very
young, and both officers of Colonel Urquhart's
regiment.

" Lord Charterhouse and Mr Cunliffe."

Mrs Traff' rose with effusion ! It was annoying, and she was exceedingly annoyed that, on the afternoon when she had such an influx of callers— worthy the name of callers, that is; for Mrs Traff' had the poorest opinion of the women-folk who are constantly dropping in about tea-time, and discussing such thoroughly feminine topics as servant-worries and housekeeping bills — her daughters should be at a tennis-party of girls only. But still, though she was annoyed, she was equal to the occasion, nor did she neglect the improvement thereof. In fact, she was civility itself.

" So strange," she said to herself, " that they should all happen to come one afternoon." But somehow it never occurred to her to think of coupling the fact with the mysterious congratulations of the old gossip Colonel Coles.

Now Lord Charterhouse, though very young, was not shy. He had been brought up in a school in which shyness does not obtain, therefore, as soon as he was comfortably established on a chair, he said that he hoped Mrs Trafford was quite well ?

" Oh ! perfectly well, thanks."

" And your daughters ? "

" Quite well, thanks. They have gone to play tennis at the Deanery."

" Oh, really ! What a pretty girl Miss Adair is ? "

"Sweetly pretty. Quite the beauty of Blank-hampton," cried Mrs Traff, in a sudden gush of charity.

"Oh! well *one* of the beauties," said Lord Charterhouse, with meaning. "You're having quite a reception—a *levée* of us this afternoon, Mrs Trafford. Orford came down with Cunliffe and me—went into Harrison's to get a pair of new gloves. By-the-bye, he *said* he was going to make a call. I should not be at all surprised if he turned up presently."

And sure enough, just as Colonel Coles was bidding the lady of the house adieu, the neat maid came in again and announced "Mr Or-ford."

Mr Orford gave a glance round the room and started visibly as he perceived who had been beforehand with him. He nodded to Colonel Coles, as that old gentleman hurried out, and, having spoken to Mrs Traff, left her to entertain Charterhouse, going himself over to where Day-rell was standing.

"Anything been said?" he asked, in a murmur.

"Yes. Coles congratulated her," Dayrell returned *sotto voce*, "and she accepted it."

"By Jove! Did you hear it?"

"No, I was too late; just by a minute, I fancy."

"Well, you had better clear out. Urquhart's coming down the High Street, and is evidently on his way here, for I asked him where he was going, and he said sharply, 'To St Eve's of course.' *I* didn't see any 'of course' about it; however that don't matter."

Then he went over and displaced Charterhouse in more ways than one; he made himself very agreeable to Mrs Traff, seeing which the others, one and all, took their departure, because, if the truth be told, each one was burning to get away and discuss the wonderful news in the outer world.

Finally Marcus Orford found himself the last of Mrs Traff's callers, to his supreme satisfaction.

"So strange," said she, "that I should have so many gentlemen in one afternoon, and so vexing my girls were out."

"Ah! I suspect they got an inkling of the truth," said he.

"Of the truth," said she innocently. "My girls?"

"No; our officers."

"Your officers! What truth? I don't quite understand, Mr Orford," she persisted, looking, poor woman, what she was, thoroughly puzzled.

"Why the news about you and Col—"

"Colonel Urquhart," announced the maid at this moment.

"D— that girl," said Orford to himself, though why she should have been the recipient of such an attention instead of the gentleman whom she announced, would be hard to say.

He looked up rather guiltily as the Colonel
entered. As for the Colonel, he nearly had a fit
on the spot from the agony of laughter which
took possession of him, and which common politeness made him suppress, although it was to the
imminent risk of his life. Perhaps, if he had
known how very near Orford had been to dis-
closing the whole truth to Mrs Traff, even to
telling her that his authority was the Colonel
himself, Urquhart would not have been so highly
amused. But then, of course, he did not happen
to know it, and everyone knows that what the
eye never sees the heart never grieves for—that
is true all the world over.

As soon as he decently could Orford betook
himself away, with an impressive leave of Mrs
Traff' and a "Good day, sir," to Urquhart, who
saw him go with another convulsion, such as
this time threatened to be too much for him.
Nor had he been left alone ten minutes with the
gratified but puzzled widow before two smart
young officers of the line regiment quartered in the
garrison, who happened to have been calling on the
Black Horse mess when Orford bounced into their
midst and blurted out the astounding news about
the commanding officer of that regiment, came
in. They were very smart boys these, much
smarter and more in the "masher" style than anything the Black Horse could boast, and each one
pulled up his collar and flattened his tie and
smoothed his sunshiny head, while the other was

saying, "How d'you do? What a charming day
it is," to Mrs Traff. Each one said, "How are
you, Colonel?" to Urquhart, and then each one
sat down, with his feet nice and flat upon the
floor, and gently rubbed the fingers of his neatly
gloved hands one against another.

"I am *so* sorry my girls are out," said she.

"Oh, we came to see *you*, Mrs Trafford," they
cried as with one breath, and then they flattened
their ties and smoothed down their curly heads
again, and awaited the development of events.

Urquhart nearly exploded.

"This is very kind of you, I'm shaw." In her
flutter of importance at this unaccustomed attention—for she had never had so much attention
at once in all her life before—Mrs Traff's accent
began to bother her again. "But I wonder if I
had no girls—"

"Oh, we knew your young ladies were not
at home," said one.

"We just met old Coles—er—Colonel Coles,
you know," with an apologetic look aside at Urquhart, as much as to say that under no circumstances would they ever dream of taking such
a liberty with his name and rank. "He—er—
told us that your young ladies were at the
Deanery."

"Yes, they are;" and Mrs Traff, although she
smiled, could have found it in her heart to wish
that the precious Deanery and all its delightful
occupants, the dear Dean, that good, sweet Lady

Margaret, and the lovely Aileen Adair, were at
Jericho, since an engagement there to practise
tennis with Miss Adair had kept her girls from
having the advantage of all this stream of visitors; under any other circumstances Mrs Traff'
would have said "a tennis party," instead of
simply saying to herself "to practise tennis'
But circumstances, of course, alter cases, and
Mrs Traff' had had enough circumstances that
afternoon, in the shape of well-looking, well-
mannered gentlemen of the fighting profession,
to alter almost any case.

And then, after a few minutes, Colonel Urquhart rose to take his departure. Mrs Traff'
rose also.

"You have not seen the dear colley, Colonel
Urquhart," she said. "He is generally here
with me," with a half-closed glance such as
made the two young gentlemen of the Blankshire Regiment look at one another with exquisite enjoyment, and then flatten their neck-
ties, as if they'd been caught stealing something
and were trying to look innocent. "Stay a
moment, and I will send for him. He is having a great romp in the garden."

So the dear colley was sent for, and came up
looking very muddy and hot, evidently having
been chasing round and round the little garden
at the back of the house in pursuit of all the
cats in St Eve's. He created quite a diversion,
for he boldly, and unchided, put his paws on to

his mistress's lap and left the marks thereof upon her best frock; he rubbed himself in a friendly sort of way up against Colonel Urquhart's new grey trousers; he thrust a wet nose and tongue into the well-gloved hand of one young officer, and made a grab at the handkerchief of the other and tore it to ribbons before it could be rescued.

"Naughty doggie," said Mrs Traff' fondly. "Never mind, he shall do as he likes, shall he not? He's such a dear, affectionate thing," she went on to Urquhart, who was trying to look as if he did not particularly mind having his clothes made as muddy as if he had been walking over the course for a red-coat race, and the day had been showery.

"Oh! very nice, very nice, he'll be a fine dog by-and-by. Wants putting into shape," he answered.

"Very fine dog," said one of the Liners, wiping his glove on the ribbons of the other's handkerchief.

"Delightful fellow," chimed in the other, flattening his tie once more.

"Well, good-bye. I will let you know to-morrow if it is at all practicable," said Mrs Traff' to Urquhart, seeing that he was getting impatient to be off.

"Thanks, thanks, very many," said he. "I shall be awfully glad if you can manage it for me."

This made the youngsters look at one another again; but if they had only known that it was merely a question of helping a poor soldier's widow in whom he was interested, they would not, perhaps, have been so intensely filled with enjoyment.

And then at last he got away, when the two young gentlemen prepared to follow his example, being, like all those who had gone before them, anxious to spread the wonderful news, and being, besides, proud of having the very latest to spread. So after a few minutes they got away, meeting on the stairs a very stout old lady, who seemed to find the steps uncommonly trying both to her age and condition.

As they let themselves out at the front door the maid opened the one upstairs and said, "Mrs Hugh Antrobus!"

Mrs Traff came forward with a chilly smile, and the words, "*That* woman" in her heart.

"Dear Mrs Traf-ford," said Mrs Hugh, "I have JUST heard the news. Let me congratulate you a *thousand* times!"

SIDELIGHT.

COLONEL URQUHART.

ON a brilliant summer's morning, years and years ago, two children sat under the shade of a huge tree whose branches spread over a noisy rippling running brook—two children, girl and boy.

"Fay," said the boy, "I'm going away to school to-morrow."

"Yes, Tom," returned the girl with a sigh, as she put an acid drop between her rosy lips.

"Who'll bring you acid drops then?" the boy persisted.

"I don't know," shaking her head.

"Who'll sharpen your pencils?" Tom asked.

But this time Fay did not speak, only shook her pretty blonde head with a desolate air too sad for words.

"Who'll get you ferns, and do your French exercises, and your sums, and string your beads," with a gesture to the coral beads round her throat, " and—and send you a valentine ? "

" You can send me a valentine, can't you, Tom ? " she asked wistfully.

" I'll try," said he sturdily.

" Perhaps Bobby Conyers will do all the rest," Fay suggested.

" I hate Bobby Conyers ! " Tom burst out passionately.

" Yes, but Bobby doesn't hate me," Fay reminded him.

What is this ?   A mere fragment of idle talk between two children ! And yet, this idle fragment struck the key-note of all Thomas Urquhart's after life. And Fay put the last golden acid drop into her mouth, then looked at him with great innocent eyes.

" Have you got any more, Tom ? " she asked.

CHAPTER X.

"QUITE A *LEVÉE.*"

AS "dear Mrs Traff-*ford!*" heard these words the stiffness of her manner somewhat relaxed, and the smile which conventional courtesy and hospitality had spread over her face became less set and slightly more friendly, if still a trifle condescending.

"Oh!"—or stay, I wish to present Mrs Traff' in exactly her own colours, so will begin again. "Ow—how d'you do? Very pleased to see you, I'm shaw! Very kind of you to congratulate me; may I ask why? What news have you heard?"

"Oh, my dear Mrs Traff-FORD," returned Mrs Hugh, with meaning, "*the* news, of *course.*"

"*The* news! I am quite in the dark."

"On your en*gage*ment," cried Mrs Hugh, "your en-*gage*-ment!"

"*Mine!*" it was the natural Mrs Traff' who

spoke then.   The gentlemen, young and old,
who had been calling upon her that afternoon
might not have known the tone, but her niece,
Madge, who knew it to a nicety, would have
recognised it in an instant.

"Yes," with a little playful laugh, as much
as to insinuate in a friendly and confidential
sort of way, a "come-don't-try-to-throw-dust-
in-my-eyes-I-know-*all*-about-it" sort of tone,
"*Yours.*"

"Mine"—in utter astonishment—"but to
whom?"

"Colonel Urquhart."

Mrs Traff' stared at Mrs Hugh for a moment
in speechless astonishment, then her mind went
back over the events of the afternoon with one
of those sudden flashes of memory such as they
say passes through the brain of a drowning man,
or of a man suddenly upset into the sea or a river.
So *this* was this meaning of it—"We have come
to see *you*, Mrs Trafford.   Oh, we knew your
young ladies were not at home;" and *this* was
what it all meant.   And then, seeing that Mrs
Hugh was beaming at her in expectation of her
reply, Mrs Traff' pulled herself together and prepared to return fire.

"Ow, de-ah, Mrs *An*-trobus, I as-shaw you
that it is *quite* prematuah!" with a pleased
simper which would have sent Urquhart, or
any other of the Black Horse officers, into a
fit on the spot.

"Oh, I heard it was all settled," in a disappointed tone; "and I had it on such *good* authority. It came to me direct from Colonel Urquhart himself."

"Yes?" Mrs Traff's tone was distinctly encouraging; in fact she wanted to learn everything she possibly could; and Mrs Hugh, delighted with her reception under the (to her) all-hallowed roof, was only too willing and glad to tell.

"I was calling on a lady just now, and Colonel Coles came; he announced it as a positive *fa-ct*. Said he had had it from Colonel Urquhart *him-self* this afternoon—at least, he corrected himself, and said he had had it from Mr OR-ford, who came into the ANTE-room of their mess and said he had just had it *from* the COLONEL himself."

"Oh," with a gratified and indulgent smile; "it is quite prematuah, I as-shaw you."

"But Colonel Coles said you had accepted his congratulations."

Mrs Traff' laughed outright.

"Oh, yes, so I did, but somebody else came in just as I said 'Thanks,' and Colonel Coles went away before I had a chance of asking what he was congratulating me about. Ow, I as-shaw you, my dear Mrs *An*-trobus, that *nothing* is settled yet."

And then Mrs Traff' asked Mrs Hugh if she would not take a cup of tea, to which Mrs

I

Hugh replied that she would take one; and over it the two ladies sat and compared notes of many things, and found out that they had much in common — which was very true, for they had indeed, a great many manners and customs particularly,— and finally Mrs Hugh went away with a proud and blissful feeling that she had made good her footing in the house of the widow Traff' for ever and for aye.

Not that Mrs Hugh spoke or thought of the little widow whom Crecy of the Yellow Horse had spoken of as "a very pushing person" in any such slighting terms. Oh, no; they say there is nobody so low but that somebody or other looks up to them, and holds them in awe and reverence. So it was with Mrs Hugh; she always, after this, spoke of the widow as "dear Mrs Traff-FORD." And this was the sort of homage which was dear to the widow's soul.

It was not long before the three girls came home from the Deanery; they had all been, and I may as well mention here that it was almost the only house in Blankhampton into which Madge Trafford ever went. And she went there because the Dean had been an old 'Varsity friend of her father's, and the Adairs simply would never take no for an answer when they invited her with the others.

"Anyone been here?" Laura asked, as soon as she reached the drawing-room.

"Yes, dears, quite a *levée* I have had," was Mrs Traff's reply. "Had you a very pleasant afternoon?"

"Pretty well; Aileen was out of sorts and rather inclined to be cross," responded Julia. "Who has been here, mother?"

"Well, Colonel Coles, and Colonel Urquhart, Mr Orford, and Mr Dayrell, and Mr Brookes," Mrs Traff' answered, ticking the names off on her fingers.

"Oh, what an awful shame! Whatever made them come to-day, I wonder? They might have known we should be out!" exclaimed Julia crossly.

"They *said* that they came to see ME," observed Mrs Traff', letting the remark drop out, as it were, unawares.

"Oh, yes, of course; but still we should like to have been at home," rejoined Julia quickly; they were very good girls on the whole, good girls and good daughters to a mother who, if a little pushing in a social sense, would always do her best to put her children as far up the ladder of success and fortune as her determined and audacious little hands could reach.

"Oh, my dear, and so should I have liked you to be at home. I really *was* vexed about it; and then Lord Charterhouse and Mr Cunliffe came."

"Oh, mother!" cried Julia and Laura in the same breath.

"And after them those two boys of the Blank-shire Regiment, Mr Owen and Mr Parsons."

" You *don't* mean it ? " cried Laura, looking ready to cry.

" Yes, I do ; and after them Mrs Antrobus."

" What ! *that* woman ? " astonished at their mother's tone.

" Well, really, dears, she is rather nice when you come to talk to her. I assure you I was most agreeably surprised."

" But what brought all the others the same day ? It's odd, isn't it ?" Julia persisted.

Madge had disappeared long before.

" Oh, my dears, I really hardly know how to tell you ; it seems so absurd ; " and certainly Mrs Traff' blushed as rosy-red from chin to brow as Laura could have done, or even a more bashful girl than Laura Trafford.

" Go on, mother ; don't keep us in suspense."

" Well, I won't. And it was just this way ; Colonel Coles came first and said something rather indefinite—as if he supposed I should know all about it—about congratulating me."

Laura Traff' drew her chair a shade nearer.

" Yes, mother ; congratulating you ; and what about ? "

' Well, that was what I was just going to ask him, when Mr Dayrell and Mr Brookes came, so of course I couldn't. I wondered and wondered, but he went away almost directly. I noticed them looking at one another, as if *something* new was going on, and then Lord Charterhouse and Mr Cunliffe came, and then Mr Orford. I

thought it was all rather odd, and presently,
when Mr Orford was the only one left, he mentioned Colonel Coles as going round to tell the
news, and I said, ' What news?' ' Oh,' said he,
' about you and Col—' I think he was going to
say Colonel somebody, but just then Colonel
Urquhart came, and Mr Orford went away immediately. And the Colonel did not stop very
long, only a few minutes after the two boys
came. And just as they were going, Mrs Antrobus came. She went straight to the point at
once, and really, it is so absurd, I hardly like to
repeat it."

" Oh, go on, mother, put us out of our misery,"
Laura implored.

" Well, it seems they are saying that I—I—
it's too absurd, you know, for anything, you
know—but it seems they are saying that I am
engaged."

" *Engaged!* " cried the girls together. " *You,*
mother ? "

" Yes. Of course, it is utterly absurd,"
modestly.

" But to whom ? "

" To Colonel Urquhart," said Mrs Traff, almost
in a whisper.

" To Col-onel Ur-quhart ! " cried Julia Traff,
in accents of the most profound astonishment.

" Is it true ? " asked Laura.

" That they are saying so—quite. And the
strange part of it all is, that Colonel Coles told

Mrs Antrobus this afternoon that he was in the Black Horse mess to-day—this afternoon, in fact —and that Mr Orford rushed in and told them the news, having come straight from the Colonel's quarters, where Colonel Urquhart had told him himself."

"Good gracious!" cried Julia Traff, over-whelmed by the tidings.

"Oh, it is perfectly absurd, of course, and out of the question altogether—I said so," cried Mrs Traff.'

"I don't see why; I think it's lovely," put in Laura.

"Oh, an old woman like me?"

"Pooh! you're not very old, mother," said Julia; "and if Colonel Urquhart likes you, I don't see that it's any business of anyone else's."

"No, perhaps not, but still—oh, it is absurd, perfectly absurd. I said so."

"Oh, but he's so nice; and think how glorious it would be for us. But, mother, didn't the others say anything about it? Didn't they offer their congratulations also?"

"No; but then they, perhaps, wouldn't like to do that, being their own colonel, would they? Not until they were quite sure," and so the Traffords, mother and daughters, talked and speculated and wondered, until at last Mrs Traff's protests that it was too utterly absurd, and not to be thought of, and absolutely out of the question, died away into pleased and smiling murmurs as she listened to her girls' chatter, which ran on and on as if the whole affair were settled, all cut and dried, and their mother about to become Mrs Urquhart, and Colonel Urquhart their stepfather, the following week.

Meanwhile, helped on its way by Colonel Coles, who had managed to cram no less than eleven calls into the time which elapsed between his leaving the Black Horse mess and the hour when most folk eat their dinner, and not retarded by Mrs Hugh, the news had spread through the old city of Blankhampton like wildfire.

And it came upon that portion of the good people of Blankhampton which constitutes " sassiety " as with a thunder-clap. Nobody could credit it, and yet it was not told as an *on dit*, but as an absolute and accomplished fact.

It happened that Captain Dayrell and young Owen of the Blankshire Regiment were among the guests gathered round the Dean's hospitable board that evening, and young Owen, confident of the truth of his tit-bit of gossip, announced it in a voice which was perfectly audible to everybody at the table. And everybody was flabbergasted! Everybody said it couldn't be true, excepting Dayrell and the boy who had let fly the thunderbolt; and seeing this, the Dean appealed to Dayrell for confirmation of his assertion that it could not be true.

Dayrell, however, was not in a position to confirm any such assertion.

"It has not been formally announced," he said, "and of course, whatever we may hear, we are not any of us in a position to ask Colonel Urquhart a question so closely concerning himself."

"But what do you think? You surely don't think it's true!" exclaimed the Dean.

"I think it is not at all improbable," said Dayrell guardedly.

I won't be quite sure, but I think the dear Dean said, "God bless my soul!" under his breath. Of course, it might have been something else, but that was what it sounded like.

Elsewhere, Colonel Coles, who had no scruples as to seeming to disregard the value of *esprit de corps*, nor the fear of committing a breach of etiquette before his eyes, was delighting a large party with a full account of the whole affair, with sundry little additions and embroideries which had grown, or been tacked on to the original fabric during the oft-repeated recital, and of which he was utterly unconscious.

And at the Black Horse mess, where the Colonel was not present, having gone to dine in the country eight miles away, it was the one topic of conversation; and the one opinion expressed was that Urquhart was suffering from mental aberration, and ought to be locked up.

SIDELIGHT.

MRS MORNINGTON-BROWN.

SHE had scarcely been so successful in Blankhampton society as Mrs Traff', principally I think because her stock of *sang froid* was not so extensive. The Mornington-Browns, mother and daughters, were certainly better-looking than the Traffords, and had more of this world's goods; but they didn't get on with Blankhampton people, chiefly because they were mean and gave themselves foolish airs.

Now it happened that the Blankhampton R.V. corps were about to give a dance, and as every single one of the officers (with the exception of the Commandant) had felt the severity of a Mornington-Brown snub—being all young men whom the M. B.'s were afraid might want to marry them—though as a matter of fact they didn't—they agreed that no invitation should be sent to them. Now the M.-B.'s wanted to

go to the ball, though they reserved to themselves the right of snubbing the givers of it,
but as they hadn't been asked, it was awkward.

But forthwith Mrs M.-B. wrote to the Commandant and asked for an invitation; he re-
ferred the matter to the committee, and, learning
the facts, wrote back that he was very sorry the
invitations were all gone.   Then a Major Morn-
ington wrote from Aldershot to the Commandant's wife asking for a card *for a friend.*
Innocently she sent it, and two days afterwards
the ball-committee received this note :—

" Mrs and the Misses M.-B. and Mr Lionel
M.-B. have the pleasure of accepting—" and
the fury of the ball-givers may be better
imagined than described.

But the M.-B.'s did not altogether get the
best of it, for when the night of the ball came
they found themselves boycotted, and the officers of the Rifle corps revenged by a single
sentence, which spread among the company
like magic :—" Oh ! by-the-bye, the Mornington-
Browns came without an invitation."

CHAPTER XI.

"ME."

BY five o'clock the following afternoon there was scarcely a single household in Blankhampton—of any social importance, that is—into which the wonderful news had not penetrated; it was upon every lip, almost, I might say, upon every countenance and in every eye; it was *the* topic of the hour.

Gin anybody at all met anybody else, he or she had a question to put, a question which was either, "Have you heard the news about Mrs Trafford?" or, "Do you think it's true that Colonel Urquhart is going to make such a fool of himself?" Yes, I admit that it was not a complimentary way of putting it, yet I am afraid—or stay, I cannot with truth say afraid, because I am perfectly sure—that such was the general way in which society regarded Colonel Urquhart's share in the latest *on dit*.

Now, society in Blankhampton had been particularly kind to him, although, on the whole, he was not a man who well requited the kind of attention of which he had so much. Perhaps, with the exception of Marcus Orford, he had more attention than any other officer in the garrison. It was natural enough; for a man who is in command of a regiment, and is rich and well-looking, is one of the most likely men in the world for mothers to make welcome in their houses.

Everybody was so kind to him. At Blankhampton Palace, which lay a mile or so outside the town, there was a spiritual lord in silken stockings and an apron, who had an extra cordial squeeze of the hand for Colonel Urquhart, which, as a rule, he kept for owners of titles and heads of great county families whose eldest sons had not yet acquired the possession of relatives by marriage : for his lordship of the holy see of Blankhamptom was very select in his company—as behoved a gentleman who had emphatically *not* been born in the purple.

It was astonishing how kind the Palace people had contrived to be in so short a time; if I were to say how many times a cover had been laid for Colonel Urquhart at the Episcopal table since the Black Horse had been quartered in the garrison, I should be accused of exaggeration, which, as a matter of fact, however many others I possess, is not one of my faults ; it was

wonderful how many and many a hamper of
fruit and game had found its way to the quarters of the rich officer who did not want these
things, passing thither by the door of many a
poor parson to whom such a gift would have
been thrice-blessed, not only because the wife's
weary load would have been lightened for that
week, but because it would have created a kindly
feeling between the one who had missed the tide
of fortune, and he who, by no great merit of his
own but rather by a lucky accident, had taken
it at the flood, and had ridden proudly on to
fame and fortune with the high and mighty
ones of the land and the income of—well, almost
a prince.

Ay, but the Lord Bish-ôp of Blankhampton
was not given to good works of that kind!
How I wish I could put him before you just
as I saw him last. Of course, my line is to
paint soldiers, so that in attempting him I may
be a little out of it; yet, he was an important
personage in that particular garrison town, so I
will try—and here goes.

He was very big, ponderous, and heavy, with
a plain-featured, square-jowled face: his admirers
were pleased to call it rugged or rough-hewn.
He had a pasty, sodden complexion, lack-lustre
eyes, with a set, dreamy, abstracted gaze; and
a tangle of unkempt, grizzled hair hung about
his ears. Add to this a manner either elabor-
ately affable or superciliously absent, and that,

I flatter myself, represents the Lord Bishop of Blankhampton to a nicety.

But although he was a very important personage in society, it cannot be said that he was often seen in the town. Perhaps he did not believe in making himself too cheap; anyway it is certain that, whilst he might frequently be heard in certain pet towns at a distance, or from the pulpit of various churches in the remote quarters of his diocese, it was but very rarely that he condescended to enlighten the inhabitants of the town from which his see took its name; and, in fact, about the only time or opportunity they had of hearing him was on the occasions of laying on of hands.

It was curious to see the effect upon those who were not prepared for the big booming voice which came from the vast presence; for the Lord Bish-ôp was wont to deliver his charge to the assembled congregation,—

Good Pee-pul!

in a voice which was in sound as a page of print looks when held under a very powerful magnifying glass, largely increased in size but somewhat blurred in outline.

Dear me, dear me, how well I remember the voice of the Lord Bishop when I was a youngster, a little chap of ten or twelve years old! It was at a confirmation held in a church which had not been selected for that ceremony before, so that the rector was new to it. The chairs—

handsome, high-backed ones, of carved black oak and crimson velvet—four of them, which always stood in the space within the rails, had been set for the attendant clergy, and after the service had begun the good rector, looking about in an agony of apprehension lest aught should go wrong, made the appalling discovery that there was not a chair at all for the Lord Bishop!

A hurried consultation with a brother parson followed, with the result that his chair was set for John, Lord Bishop of the Diocese. But the rector, good, hospitable soul, came to the rails at the side and beckoned the churchwarden, who in turn beckoned the old woman who cleaned the church, and she—bless her—dived into an adjacent vestry, and came out a minute later radiantly triumphant with a splendid specimen of a wooden rush-bottomed chair. This was seized and hoisted overhead from one to another till it reached the rails, and in another moment would have disappeared behind the voluminous white robes of the parson who had given up his chair, so that he might still be able to sit down when needful.

Unfortunately the leaden gaze of the Lord Bish-ôp turned upon the homely and unpretending rush-bottomed piece of furniture, humble but not tainted by the pomp and vanities of this wicked world, and he said, in an awful voice,—

"Take away that chair!"

To my childish imagination the command, with

its attendant gesture, was a paraphrase of a more celebrated utterance,—"Take away that bauble!"

So the rush-bottomed chair was hoisted up aloft once more, and carried away to oblivion, followed by the shining eyes of all the youthful covenanters. Can we blame them? Perhaps not ; yet the awful voice boomed out again,—

"You will attend to ME!"

Upon my word, it was the biggest ME I have ever heard before or since.

But these are childish memories, and altogether by the way ; my business is with the way in which Blankhampton society accepted the news of the reported engagement between Colonel Urquhart and Mrs Trafford. As I said, the Palace people had been exceptionally kind to him ; so, indeed, had those at the Deanery, not because the dear Dean—most people called him the dear Dean, though I never did hear a single soul say the same of the Bishop—wished to get rid of his beautiful daughter, but simply because he wasn't going to be outdone in that kind of hospitality by the Bishop.

So, indeed, *all* the heads of the principal households in the town or neighbourhood had been, some from one reason, some from another, yet all with the same result.

And this was the end of it all, that he should fall a victim to the little pert-nosed widow whom the very best people, like Crecy of the Yellow Horse, were wont to term a very pushing little person !

SIDELIGHT.

THE DAMERELS.

THEY were remarkably fine girls, well grown, and blessed with the best of health, with faces prettier than common, and complexions that were dazzling in the beauty of their rose and lily tints.

Perhaps they were a shade heavy in build—what their detractors were able to term " very coarse," without running the risk of being called anything worse than ill-natured; but to most eyes their redundance of person had something very bonny about it, and on the whole they were greatly admired.

It happened one day that the subject of their looks came in question at the club, when said Godfrey Mauleverer, *àpropos* of Elizabeth Damerel, " Oh! she's a very good-looking girl, of course, but it's a pity she deals so largely in pocket-handkerchiefs," and as he spoke, he laid

his hand upon his—I had almost said *manly*,
but we will compromise matters and say his
masculine bosom —just where redundance is
considered a beauty in the fair sex, and the
soul of one Lester Brookes fairly boiled within
him.

He didn't like Elizabeth Damerel—indeed, he
was accustomed to particularise her as *that*
Elizabeth—but all the same he thought right
was right.

"I don't know, I'm sure, anything about
pocket handkerchiefs," he said curtly, "but
there are *some* young ladies in Blankhampton
who would be improved if they did a little
more at that kind of thing," and then Mr
Mauleverer suddenly remembered that his own
sisters were—well slender.

CHAPTER XII.

FACE TO THE —— ENEMY.

"IT is incredible!" cried Lady Mainwaring to her nieces, the two Damerel girls. "If it had been one of the girls it would be easy enough to understand, but *Mrs Trafford herself!* Well, it is simply as absurd as if *I* were to marry him."

"No, auntie dear," cried the elder of the Damerels, "it would be easy enough to understand Colonel Urquhart marrying *you*, but Mrs Trafford—well, it is simply ridiculous. She is old enough to be his mother."

"Hardly that; but more than old enough to be his stepmother without accusing his father of making a very foolish second marriage in point of age," returned Lady Mainwaring, who was a cold-eyed, passionless sort of woman, without any warmth of manner, except on paper,

when, if it suited her purpose, she could be
gushing, and often was. "However, it really is
no business of ours, my dears; if Colonel Urquhart *likes* to marry his—his stepmother, he must
please himself; and, after all, the marriage will
take her away from Blankhampton, which, as
she has three girls to take about, will be rather
a good thing. Besides, a colonel's wife will be
rather an advantageous person to know, and—
er—I think I shall get the first refusal of her
house. I have been wanting to get into St
Eve's for some time. I was exceedingly annoyed that Mrs Berkeley died whilst I was
abroad. I always intended to have her house,
though I did not quite like to bespeak it when
there was a possibility of her recovering."

Most of the girls who had admired Colonel
Urquhart said, "*What* a shame!" and most of
their mothers returned, "He must be mad!"
and as the day wore on and the report was not
contradicted, but spread further and further,
most of the men who had asked in the morning, "Do you think it's true that Colonel Urquhart is going to make such a fool of himself?"
now simply accepted the statement as a fact, and
said, "What an ass!"

Mrs Traff' herself remained indoors, not being
minded to face the storm of questions and congratulations which she knew would assail her;
but her girls went out in the morning and
braved the gossip of a whole town, admitting

nothing, declaring they had heard nothing of the affair, and yet by their very denials confirming the story more than if they had told the truth. And in the afternoon they went off to a tennis-party five miles away, leaving their mother in the house, but "not at home" to any callers excepting Colonel Urquhart.

And at four o'clock, a few minutes after the hour had struck, Colonel Urquhart was seen by a dozen or more quizzing pairs of eyes upon the broad steps of No. 7 St Eve's, and immediately a fresh impetus was given to the story, and it went on its way rejoicing.

"I tell you, my dear," said one blooming girl who had so seen him, "I saw him come up to the door. I was standing close to the house talking to Beatrice Bannerman, and we saw him come swinging up St Eve's, and turn in at No. 7. He hammered at the door with five or six knocks, and stood tapping his foot with his stick, and looking so gloriously happy that I really shouldn't wonder at anybody falling over head and ears in love with him."

"Well, I can *not* understand it," said "my dear" with decision. "No, I cannot."

But undoubtedly Colonel Urquhart did call on Mrs Traff' that afternoon, the reason being that during the morning a note was brought to him by hand.

"DEAR COLONEL URQUHART.—Can you call

on me this afternoon about four o'clock? I
particularly want to see you.—Very truly yours,
"MARION TRAFFORD."

So when, after the little scene described above,
Colonel Urquhart was shown into the pretty
drawing-room at No. 7, he found the widow
Traff' all by herself, with rose-coloured blinds
judiciously lowered, a pretty lace trifle dotted
here and there, with pink ribbons perched
coquettishly on the top of the strange-looking
erection of padded plaits with which she adorned
her head, and a dainty handkerchief trimmed
with lace and embroidery tucked carelessly into
the bosom of her dress.

She really did not look half bad, only—alas!
alas! for the endeavours of frail humanity—in
spite of all these attractions, with the addition
of a good deal of pearl powder and just a
touch of rouge, the little perky nose was still
there—not only the little perky nose, but also
the high-pitched cracked voice; and, unfortunately, emotion or excitement sent the accent all
astray.

"Ow, Colonel Urquhart! Ow-de-ah! You
must have thought it very strange for me to
send for you; but—but—er—"

"I suppose you have got the grant?" said he,
alluding to the case of the poor widow in whom
they were both interested.

Mrs Traff' gave a great start.

" Ow—no—it was not that at all. Ow—no
—I," with a great sigh, "I am very much dis-
turbed. I asshaw you, Colonel Urquhart, I have
not slept all night, and—and, in fact, I am quite
in trouble."

" Yes ? What is the matter? Can I help
you in any way ? " said he kindly. He really
thought the little woman had got herself into
a scrape of some kind. "If I can be of the
least service to you, pray command me."

" Well, really, I hardly know how to tell you,"
hanging her head in quite a coquettish way.

Urquhart, however, was not a man open to
this kind of thing, and stood bolt upright in
front of her, looking so big and soldierly that
Mrs Traff' began to feel a little frightened.

" Really ? Oh, pray go on," said he, in a cold-
blooded tone.

" Well, you know how people will talk. Indeed, I always say that Blankhampton is the
most outrageously gossipping place I was ever
in—and—and—really, Colonel Urquhart, it is
most embarrassing for me to tell you all this.
Yet what am I to do ? " spreading out her hands
—they were little hands—with a delightfully
childish air of helplessness.

" Oh, don't mind me ; go on," said Urquhart
bluntly.

" Well—er— Really, it is most awkward for
me, but I suppose I must tell you outright.
People are actually saying that—that—you and

I are—" there was a long pause, and then the
widow let fall, in a meek and humble voice, not
like her voice at all, but like the echo of some
soft sigh, one single word, " *engaged* " !

For one moment Urquhart was convulsed.   He
turned from pink to scarlet and scarlet to crimson and from crimson to a fine royal purple ; but
he was an officer and a gentleman, and, moreover,
a very gallant specimen of his class, so somehow
or other he choked the convulsion down, and
kept a brave and calm front to the—I very
nearly said enemy, but of course I meant lady.
Besides, a very uncomfortable sensation flashed
into his mind as he remembered his conversation
with Marcus Orford,—when he had said, with
a grim sense of joking, that Mrs Traff' might
do worse—that he had been to blame for this.
What an ass he had been to set such a tale
afloat, for without the shadow of a doubt he
had set it afloat, though unintentionally.

"And the worst of it is," murmured the
widow in a plaintive voice, " that several people
have told me that they had it straight from
you ; and yesterday," with a piteous intonation,
" almost *all* your officers called here, and though
I was puzzled to think what could have brought
so many of them, I had not the least idea until
late in the afternoon, when a lady called and
told me she had it straight from you."

" Dear me, dear me ! I'm awfully sorry !" exclaimed Urquhart—and so he was.   "I assure

you, Mrs Trafford, I couldn't be more annoyed
if—if they had said I was engaged to my gran
—at least, I mean—" breaking off short and
fairly biting the word in two, "at least, I—I
am awfully annoyed—awfully annoyed. Really,
'pon my word!" floundering hopelessly in search
of a correct way of expressing himself, "at least,
I hope you won't be so awfully angry as to cut
me over it, though it's enough to make you, it
is indeed."

"It is dreadful for me ; so embarrassing," the
little widow murmured plaintively. "In my
position, quite unprotected as I am, and with
my girls, it is a most painful position to be
placed in, most painful, I asshaw you."

"Of course it is ; of course, I quite understand
that," cried Urquhart, who was beginning to have
a fellow feeling for Mrs Traff' such as no other
means on earth could have brought about ; and
then he began walking up and down the room
with long, hasty strides, trying with all the
ingenuity of his clever brain to think of some
decent and gentlemanlike way out of it. What
the devil was he to do? his thoughts ran, as
he marched to and fro. And oh! confound it,
if the little widow wasn't beginning to pipe her
eye! Well, poor little soul, it was no wonder,
that d—d long tongue of Orford's had brought
her enough vexation to upset any woman.

"Mrs Trafford," he exclaimed, suddenly coming to a standstill as a brilliant idea struck him,

"I only see one way out of it. There is only one thing for us to do."

"And that," said the widow, raising her head, her heart beating loud and fast, "and that is—?"

"For you to say that you refused me," said Colonel Urquhart solemnly.

For one moment the disappointment was almost too great for words; the realisation of the truth was almost too crushing. It was not, for I do not wish to do the little widow the smallest injustice, it was not that she had any fancy or particular liking for him, not that she had really any wish to marry him or anybody else; only it had come upon her so unexpectedly, it had come straight from him. And he was a man whom she or any other woman would be proud to call husband; perhaps, with the exception of Marcus Orford, she would have chosen him for one of her girls before any other man in the world.

And although she had not professed to admit the possibility of such a marriage ever coming to pass, the speculations and merry-making of her girls over the prospect had been very pleasant to her. It would have been such a position for them, they would have had such chances of settling well, and what she considered suitably. Oh! without doubt, it was a bitter moment when the cup which had seemed to be brimful and running over with triumph and happiness was dashed from her lips by the band which she believed to have held it there.

"For you to say that you refused me," said Urquhart, in his most solemn voice.

By an effort Mrs Traff' pulled herself together, and looked him and the situation fairly in the face.

"I could not do that," she said bluntly. All the little girlish airs of coquetry and embarrassment had vanished, and she stood upright now before him, looking him straight in the eyes, the cool, calculating woman of the world once more. "Oh! I could not do that."

"Why?" with a crestfallen look, and an accent of intense disappointment.

"Because nobody would believe me. No," raising her hand, "I don't mean to pay you any compliment, but simply because, if you had asked me such a question and I had refused you, I should not speak of it to anyone. No lady would!"

"You are right. I don't know what to do," he said hopelessly.

If she had been a less clever woman, she would have said at that moment, "Make it true!" But Mrs Traff' was wise in her day and generation. She had been too many years in the world, since she had been left to do her best for her girls, to make such a mistake, even though the temptation was the strongest she had ever suffered in all her life. Instead, she conquered

it, and rose triumphant, and began to talk about
" her time of life."

" It is a very dreadful thing for me," she said,
in an unhappy voice ; " in my position, with my
girls, and at my time of life.   It is very cruel,
whoever has set the story afloat ; and, really, it
is strange how *every*body persists that they had
the authority for it straight from *you*.   I shall
be the laughing-stock of the town, the most
gossipping, scandal - loving town in England.
It is really very cruel, and I do not feel I
have done *any*thing to deserve it.   I do not
indeed."

Colonel Urquhart began to ask himself if he
was not the biggest villain unhung.   Here had
he, without the slighest intention, certainly—
though what difference did intention make if the
result was the same ?—but here had he, just to
gratify a grim sense of humour, made a statement with an air of reality which was calculated
to deceive nine persons out of ten into believing
words which carried a joke upon the very face
of them !   What on earth should he, could he
do ?   For one wild moment he was almost
desperate enough to say, " Let us end it in the
one way which will effectually stop all gossip.
Let us marry ! " but, fortunately for him, and
unfortunately for Mrs Traff', he happened to look
at her just then, and the look was sufficient.
No, come what might, come what would, he
could not stand that.   It was altogether useless

and out of the question to think of that as a way out of the difficulty.

Then light flashed into his brain and cleared up everything.

"Mrs Trafford," said he, "*I* will say you refused me. I will put the question to you, and you say no; and then I will say freely that you refused me. Nobody will disbelieve me. Surely *that* cannot do you any harm."

"No, I don't know that it would," hesitatingly.

"Mrs Trafford," said he promptly, "will you marry me?"

Mrs Trafford gasped for breath. How utterly this man was now in her power. What if she said "YES"?

He was looking eagerly at her in his desire to atone for the trouble and annoyance which his thoughtless joke had brought upon her. Then happily good sense got the upper hand, and she answered, "No!" But surely never in all the history of this wide world, never did a woman say "No" so unwillingly before.

"Thank you," said he humbly.

SIDELIGHT.

THE WIFE OF THE LORD BISHÔP.

THE wife of the Lord Bishôp was standing in the centre of a group of admiring ladies, chiefly the wives of lesser lights of the great Church Militant, who in their best bibs and tuckers were doing honour to an episcopal entertainment.

Now it happened that a certain great Personage had been staying at the Palace, who, on leaving, had presented the wife of the Lord Bishôp with a diamond bracelet as a souvenir of the visit; and this bracelet was now being displayed to the admiring eyes of half a score of ladies, to whose portion such worldly vanities as diamond bracelets did not come, with very pardonable pride by the wife of the Lord Bishôp.

She was a handsome woman, with a little trick of turning her face sideways and drooping her eyelids over eyes which were certainly out of the common beautiful, and she smiled and bridled, and turned her face so as to show her profile, more as if the pretty bauble had been a golden crown to wear in the Heavenly Jerusalem than mere dross of earth: and all her less fortunate sisters envied her, until a handsome old parson standing by, exclaimed,—

" Oh! great Personages carry that sort of things about in their pockets to give to anyone they meet; there's no great kindness in it. It's the proper thing for them to do."

As the jovial, contented tones fell upon her ear, the Bishop's wife shivered, and the Lord Bishop standing near her said to himself,—

" If only I hadn't posted that letter this morning offering him Routh."

But the letter was gone, and Routh was worth fifteen hundred a year!

CHAPTER XIII.

THE BEST OF THE BARGAIN.

TRULY Mrs Trafford was a clever little woman. She watched him go across the street, and then she pulled her blinds up to their proper level, that is to say, the height at which she usually kept them; then she went into her bedroom and changed her pretty head-dress for a more ordinary one, put the bit of lace and embroidery which stood in place of a handkerchief away in a drawer, and passed a well-soaped sponge ruthlessly over the pretty pink and white complexion which had made her for an hour or two look quite girlish. And when she had done all this she went back into her drawing-room and rang for her afternoon tea.

"Cox," she said to the maid who brought it —she always called her servants "Cox," or "Jones," or some such name, it sounded better than the less pretentious Mary or Jane—"oh, Cox, you need not say anyone called this afternoon."

"Very well, ma'am," returned Cox, outwardly quite passionless, inwardly eaten alive by curiosity to know what could be the meaning of such an order.

But neither by expression nor gesture did Mrs Traff' betray herself, and Cox had to go down to her fellow-servant as wise as she had come. And then Mrs Traff' put her feet on the fender and began to read the third volume of the last novel, eating her buttered toast with a keen appetite, and sipping her tea with relish. And after that, being a plucky little woman, she put on her things and went out, meeting a great many people whom she knew, and receiving many congratulations. She received all the latter with the same expressions of amusement.

"I and Colonel Urquhart going to be married! Oh! how absurd. I asshaw you it is quite a mistake; oh! quite. I never entertained such an idea for a moment. As if it is likely at *my* time of life."

"It really sounds," remarked one dear friend to another, "as if there had been something in it, and yet it seems such an unlikely thing for a man like Colonel Urquhart to do."

"It is a queer affair altogether," rejoined the other. "If there was nothing in it, how could such a tale get afloat?"

"Oh! my dear, that is easy enough. How did the tale get into the newspapers that a marriage had been arranged between the Bishop's daughter and the Rev. Bertie Capel? Why, the Palace people put it in, of course; *every*body knew how delighted they would have been if Bertie Capel had only *looked* at her."

"And Bertie Capel didn't see it?"

"Bertie Capel wanted to better himself when he married, and did it," laughed the other. "However, I shall make an effort to get at the truth when I see Colonel Urquhart. I have asked him to dine on Sunday on purpose."

And when the Sunday and dinner-time came the good lady did so, for she immediately told Urquhart that she had heard that she was to congratulate him.

"Unfortunately no," said Urquhart, in his most solemn tones, and with his most imperturbable manner.

"Why unfortunately? I don't understand," exclaimed the puzzled seeker after truth.

"Because, though I asked Mrs Trafford to do me the honour of becoming my wife, I am sorry to say she refused me."

"And, my dear," said she, when she repeated the conversation to her dear friend, "the man was evidently speaking the literal truth. I am quite sure he is mad, perfectly mad."

"What in the world," said the other, "*can* he have seen in Mrs Trafford?"

That was what most people asked themselves and one another when the story had flown round Blankhampton sufficiently to be pretty generally known. But the secret never oozed out, and Colonel Urquhart kept it for ever.

Marcus Orford, when he heard it, went straight to him and said,—

"Urquhart, is this true I hear about you?"

"I don't know at all! What have you heard?" Urquhart answered, looking up from his book.

"That Mrs Trafford refused you."

"Oh, yes, it's true enough," speaking indifferently.

"But you don't mean to say you asked her?"

"Yes, I did."

"To marry you?" Orford persisted.

"Yes, to marry me!"

"Urquhart," said Orford solemnly, "if I were you—no, you needn't be offended, in fact, I'm sure you won't, for you know we have always been good friends—but if I were you I would just go straight up to town and see a first-rate doctor. Not a nobody, but someone who thoroughly understands *brains!* For, seriously, I don't think if you were altogether *yourself* such an idea would ever have entered your mind."

"Oh! shut up," returned Urquhart impatiently.

"Yes, I know, but—" Orford began.

"I won't stand much more of your cheek,'

broke in Urquhart. "Mrs Trafford refused me,
and that's enough. I don't want to hear any
more about it."

"Mrs Trafford showed her good sense, and, by
Jove! I respect her more than I ever could have
thought possible!" Orford cried.

"And so do I; and don't you think, my friend,
that we've had about enough of the subject for
to-day?" asked Urquhart grimly.

"Yes; but, Urquhart, I would go and see
that doctor. I would indeed," Orford urged.

"If your brains were as sound as mine it
would be a good thing for you," returned the
Colonel coolly.

"Perhaps so; but all the same, I would—"
and then Orford, being near the door, went out
suddenly in order to avoid a boot-jack which
went sailing through the air in his direction,
and hit the door just at the level where his face
had been a moment before.

When he was gone Urquhart lay back in his
chair and laughed till the tears stood in his
eyes. And in the corridor outside Orford stood
shaking his head dolefully.

"Well, I've been all these years in the Black
Horse with Urquhart, and d— me if I don't
believe he's got softening of the brain, or something of that kind. Urquhart of all people.
Why, bless my soul, I'd almost sooner it was
my own father. Fancy any fellow *wanting* to
marry Mrs Traff'?"

SIDELIGHT.

SIR ANDREW HAMILTON.

HE was undoubtedly one of the most popular generals who had ever been in command of a district. Not like some, who are popular everywhere except in their own commands, on the principle, perhaps, that "a prophet is not without honour save in his own country."

And his was a charming character; one he had worked hard to gain, and had to work harder to keep. Even among "the unco' guid" he had the reputation of being a really godly man, and in the cause of charity right diligently did he air his uniform on all occasions. It might be for Wesleyan bazaar; for the opening of the local exhibition; for Congregationalist concert, or the fancy fair of the Church institute. Or it might be for the distribution of prizes at the School of Art, or for the amateur theatricals of the Y. M. C. Association. It was all one to him; he was sure to be there, and might be counted on for an effective speech, in which the words "and beat our swords into the plough-shay-ah, and our spe-ahs into the pruning-hook," would as certainly occur as a quotation from "dear George Herbert" would form part of the Archdeacon's sermon when he ascended the Parish pulpit.

But by-and-by promotion came, and Sir Andrew's place knew him no more. On the 6th he gave over his command; on the 7th the new general appeared in public for the first time, and gave away the prizes to the boys of the Ragged School; this was his first speech :—

"I would have you to know that I am always ready to help you with my presence, my advice, and my influence. But I am not a rich man like Sir Andrew Hamilton, and I have a large family—therefore I have no money to give you."

Yes, this was his first speech; it was also his last.

CHAPTER XIV.

A COSY CHAT.

BY way of showing his appreciation of Mrs Traff's good sense, Marcus Orford called upon her the following afternoon, and finding her alone and just about to begin her afternoon tea and hot buttered toast, accepted with thanks her offer of a fresh relay for him, and settled himself down to spend a cosy, chatty hour with her. It was not a little surprising how his feelings had changed towards her during the past week—from calling her "the old cat," or "the widow Traff'," he had come to saying "the little woman down in St Eve's"; and in nine cases out of ten, if not actually the whole of the half score, when a man begins to speak or think of a lady as "the little woman," his liking for her has increased enormously.

Mrs Traff' was very kind and nice to him.

"Is there any news, Mr Orford?" she asked, as she handed him a cup of tea.

"Well, the General's got promotion, and has to give up his appointment," he answered.

"Oh, dear, I *am* sorry; there will never be another general like Sir Andrew."

"No; he's a very good fellow. It's a pity though he has such a weakness for his uniform."

"Why? Do you know, we think he looks so nice in it."

"Yes, so he may; but then, you see, he makes us all wear ours everywhere, which is a great nuisance. An order went out this morning that nobody is to appear at the Archdeacon's garden party except in uniform."

"You don't mean it?" cried Mrs Traff.

"Well, not in so many words; but nobody is to appear in public out of uniform before sundown—that is, six o'clock."

"But how about you?" glancing at his light biscuit-coloured clothes.

"Oh, I?" looking down at his long legs and smart patent leather boots. "Oh, well, I came in a cab, you know."

"But why don't you like your uniform? I'm sure you all look very nice in it."

"It's uncomfortable—and conspicuous—and stiff—and—and it's so awfully expensive. One couldn't go into a lady's drawing-room in one's shabbiest things, and to wear one's best every day would be simply ruinous. It's all very well, you know, for Sir Andrew—he is as rich as a Jew; but for a man like me, whose father only allows him a bare sufficiency, it's quite a different thing. However, the next man has ten or twelve children, and I daresay will have more mercy on our pockets."

" Ah! I never thought about that," murmured the widow, handing the plate of toast to him.

" Thanks," helping himself. " What good toast you have, Mrs Trafford. Yes, awfully good; it's a thing our mess rather fails in, particularly if we want it in our own rooms. Yes, it's a long way to bring it, of course, and it gets cold on the journey; but if you want to give an afternoon tea you don't think of that —you only think it's a nuisance. By-the-bye, I hope you intend to patronise our sports, Mrs Trafford."

" The regimental sports? When are they?"

" The 17th, I believe; they're to be awfully good this year. I hope you mean to come, and bring your young ladies."

" Oh, I should like to come immensely, and so, I am sure, would they," Mrs Trafford answered.

" Then may I hope you will do me the honour. I have two good rooms, four windows; about the best for seeing, I think."

" Oh, thank you very much. We shall enjoy it immensely—my daughters and I, that is. My niece will be away."

"Oh! she is going away?"

Mrs Traff did not notice the crestfallen tone.

"Yes; she goes the day before to stay with some old friends of her father's in Midland-shire."

"Yes," Orford put in, hope springing up anew in his manly bosom, for in Midlandshire was situate one of his father's country houses, by name Garforth Grange, and at Garforth there was always a sufficient staff of servants for any of the family to stay in the house at any time, no matter how short the notice. "What part of Midlandshire?"

"Near Newton Amshurst; some people called St Maur. I do not know them at all, but Madge is exceedingly intimate with one of the daughters. We have asked her here several times, but she has always been prevented from coming. Laura, however, has been asked to visit her."

"And Miss Laura is not going this time!" he asked, in such a tone of anxiety that the lady, who was not a fool or even slow of under-standing by any means, could not help but notice it, and said to herself in no small sur-prise that, after all, it was not Julia, but her youngest flower, Laura, who was the most at-tractive person at No. 7 St Eve's to this eligible and attractive officer of dragoons.

"Oh, no, my girls have never been there; in fact, we have never seen these St Maurs," she made haste to answer; then added, with her

very own little careless air of being able to
sum up her neighbours and settle their weight
and position in society in three words without
the faintest fear of being at fault, " But I believe they are very good people ; my niece says
they are charming, and I am glad for her to go
to them, for she has never cared to go out here.
After a life in town with an artist father, of
course, she does not find a place like Blankhampton very amusing. So I am very glad for
her to visit her father's old friends."

Mrs Trafford did not think it necessary to
add that she was only too glad to take the fullest
advantage of her niece's disinclination to enter
much into Blankhampton society, considering
that two girls were more than sufficient for one
little woman, who had hard work to make both
ends meet so as to cover the necessary round
of visiting and entertaining, to dress suitably,
and take them everywhere. But she was not
any degree less honest than the Honourable
Marcus Orford himself, sitting over there in
his easy chair with his cup of fragrant tea and
a beautiful slice of hot buttered toast (a piece
off the relay plate), for he said quietly, " Oh,
yes, the St Maurs are very nice people," not
thinking it at all necessary to add beyond the
fact that he had knowledge of the St Maurs of
Newton Amshurst, the information that he had
known them from his childhood up, root and
branch, or that they had been on the terms of

closest intimacy with the Orfords from generation to generation.

"Oh! you know them?" cried Mrs Traff', only
too pleased to find there was even this slight
connecting link between her belongings and
him.

"Oh, yes. Which of the girls is Miss Trafford's
particular friend?"

"Norah."

"Oh, Norah! Yes; she's a nice girl. I like
Maud the best myself."

Mrs Traff' heard and took note of his tone of
utter indifference with feelings of intense satisfaction, for, as she said to herself, there was
evidently nothing to be feared from that quarter;
by "feared" she of course meant no probability of one of the St Maurs girls marrying
Marcus Orford, and becoming in time Lady
Ceespring.

"I rather think I shall be going away for a
few days myself at the end of the month, if I
can get leave, that is," he said vaguely.

"Yes? Are you going to Scotland?"

"Oh, no. I want to go home."

So he did, if by going home he meant into
Midlandshire, although his father and mother
seldom or never went to Garforth Grange.

"Oh, yes," and then somehow Mrs Traff' rather
came to a standstill for want of a subject.

Orford, however, helped himself to another
piece of toast and started one.

"Do you know Mrs Antrobus?" he asked abruptly.

Mrs Traff' started a little.

"Er—yes—er—a little—er—*very* slightly—very slightly in-*deed!*"

"Ah, I thought perhaps you might know her pretty well—know all about her, you know."

"Ow, no!"

In her flurry the accent went all wrong again; for Mrs Traff', since the pleasurable excitement of Mrs Hugh's congratulations had passed off, had somewhat repented herself of her affable manner towards that stout and friendly lady. Like many another cute but lonely little widow woman, Mrs Traff' went on the principle that it was worse than foolish to be intimate with people who were neither use nor ornament: it is a wise plan, and even those who do not care to follow it, cannot but admit the wisdom of such a course.

"Ah! then you don't know anything about her?"

"Nothing at all, except that I met her at Lady Mainwaring's, who is a little—er—er—well, a little rash in her introductions; she called here once, but—er—I really don't know anything more about her, nothing *at all.*"

"Oh, I see. Well, I don't know that I particularly want to know anything about her. By-the-bye, wasn't her daughter engaged to Eliot Cardella at one time?"

"I really cannot say. We had not come here at the time the Cuirassiers were here. Mr Cardella was in the Cuirassiers, was he not?"

"Yes, and died out in India of fever."

"Ah, yes, yes. I remember; very sad, it was. I *felt* so for dear Lady Mallinbro', poor thing."

"Yes, yes; it was an awful pity. Poor Eliot was one of the best fellows in the world. By-the-bye, she seems to be a good deal admired—Miss Antrobus, I mean."

"Oh, yes, very much indeed." Mrs Traff's tone was like ice, but she was far too wise a little woman to do worse for the fair Polly than damn with faint praise. "A very pretty face it is, very pretty."

"Yes; can't say I particularly admire that type myself," returned Orford, "but of course she's awfully pretty, there's no denying it. In fact a man told me the other day if he only had some money he should go for Miss Antrobus."

"One of your regiment?" Mrs Traff inquired blandly.

"Oh, dear no; I haven't heard much about her from any of our officers; I believe Charterhouse is rather intimate with them. By-the-bye, Mrs Trafford, have you heard about the Leslies? Do you know them?"

"I have met them several times. No, I've not heard anything about them."

" They've had their house burnt down."

" You don't say so ! What ! Primrose Bank ? "

Orford nodded.

" Yes, burnt down to the very ground."

" You *don't* mean it. Ow, *poor* things."

Mrs Traff' was obliged to get a little excited over this, though she didn't know the Leslies, and her meeting them meant in church and such like places of general congregation.

" Yes, it's quite true. Our officers are wondering whether they'll take some place in the country, or whether they'll come to live in Blankhampton. The latter they hope, as they are such uncommonly pretty girls."

" Ow, de-ah, I should not think Blank-hampton would suit them at all," said Mrs Traff' rather acidly, for Blankhampton had quite enough girls of all sorts to her mind without being in any way benefited by the addition of a large family of fair, handsome, well-grown, popular girls such as the Leslies were.

" Perhaps not," in a tone of such supreme indifference that the little widow woman's hopes began to rise again.

Finally Marcus Orford betook himself away with a renewed promise from Mrs Traff' to come on the 17th and witness the interesting lambs of the Black Horse strive in the merry tug-of-war, race the quarter mile, run the mile itself, scramble over hurdles and under poles, jump in sacks, and generally make merry.

"It will be charming, charming!" cried Mrs Traff', with effusive delight and a little touch of the accent. "So very kind of you to ask us."

"So very kind of you to come," he returned gallantly.

SIDELIGHT.

LORD CEESPRING.

THE Honourable Marcus Orford went to mess one night when nearly all his brother-officers had assembled in the ante-room.

"Why, Mr Winks," he exclaimed, "I didn't know you were back! How did you leave everyone at Coombe?"

"All pretty well, I think," answered Mr Winks, otherwise Lord Charterhouse.

"And who was there?" Orford went on.

"Your people, amongst others."

"Really! oh! I didn't know they were going there. And how did you get on with my governor?"

Mr Winks pulled a long face, and shook his head dolefully.

"Hey!" said Orford. "Didn't you and he hit it off?"

. Mr Winks shook his head again.

"Hit it off?" he repeated. "Why, ⟨ put him into such a rage last night at dinner, I thought he'd have had a fit on the spot. And what the devil I said to offend him, I'll be hanged if I know. I just asked him a simple question; but there—"

"No, no; go on. Nobody knows his little ways better than I do. Go on. What did he do?"

"Smashed his plate; chucked his knife and fork into the fireplace; d—d the servants—oh! yes, it was after the ladies had gone — and asked me if I wanted to insult him? But what the devil he meant, I—don't —know!"

"Well? What then?" with a roar of laughter.

"Oh! I told him so; and then he calmed down a bit, and said he'd been hasty; quite thought I meant to be personal—though what on earth what there could be *personal* in my asking him if he knew who was going to stand on the Liberal side for Warnecliffe—"

"You never did?" cried Brookes.

"You *don't* mean it?" laughed Dayrell.

"Yes, but I did," asserted Mr Winks, wondering why Orford had gone into a convulsion of laughter which quite prevented speech.

"Good heavens! Don't you know," Dayrell asked, "that our friend, Lord Ceespring, is the

most absolutely conservative Tory in England
—in England, *on earth*—and that Archie Falconer once put Orford here up for that very
honour, and brought his father down with the
family doctor to find out whether he was mad
or not? Didn't you know *that*? Bless the boy,
what a lot you have to learn."*

.   .   .   .

"Did ye 'ear that, Bill?" said one of the
mess-waiters in a whisper to a comrade a few
minutes later. "By gum! but 'e must be a nice
old cup o' tea."

* See "A Regimental M.P." ("In Quarters," by J. S. W.)

CHAPTER XV.

A GLIMMER OF TRUTH.

JUST outside the house he happened to run against Urquhart.

"Oh, I say, Urquhart," he blurted out, "I want a fortnight's leave. Do you think—"

"I think you've had an awful lot of leave of late, my friend," returned Urquhart grimly.

"Yes; but, Urquhart, it's no shamming this time, it's real necessity," Orford urged.

"Well, you'd better put in for it."

"Thanks, awfully," gratefully.

"Where are you going?"

"Home," answered Orford promptly.

"Really?"

"Yes, really. I say, are you going to Mrs Traff's?"

"Certainly not. No use wasting time there. Mrs Traff' won't have anything to say to me," said Urquhart. "I suppose I must look out elsewhere."

"Yes. By Jove! I say, I'd no idea she was such a nice little woman. I've been sitting with her this last hour. 'Pon my soul I thought you pretty nearly a lunatic a day or two ago, but positively I'm not so much surprised at you after all. By Jove! no; a man ten or fifteen years your senior might do very well, might do a devilish deal worse, upon my soul he might."

"Than do what?" asked a voice beside him, and Orford turning round saw Lester Brookes at his elbow.

"Than marry Mrs Traff," answered Orford promptly. "There's that hoary old sinner Coles, for instance. Gad, what a wife she'd make for him!"

"Yes, that's so; she certainly would. But I don't suppose she'd look at him," with a diffident glance from under his eyelashes at the Colonel.

"Not she. Well I must be off," said Urquhart, and with a nod left his juniors standing together.

They stood and watched him go along St Eve's till he passed out of sight with a steady soldierly, swinging tramp. Neither of them, not even Orford, who knew him as well as any man or woman in the world, guessed aught of the convulsion of laughter which

possessed him, nor how, when he had safely
turned the corner, he stood still to laugh,
causing the young lady who had seen him
go into No. 7, when she was chatting to
Beatrice Bannerman, to wonder if that handsome Colonel Urquhart was not an utter and
hopeless lunatic.

But, bless the dear child, not a bit of it; Urquhart was as sane as herself at that moment:
only the idea of old Coles, the gossip, being
wedded to Mrs Traff', and Lester Brookes'
modest and diffident look combined, had simply
been too much for him, that was all.

And Marcus Orford and his comrade were
still standing under the windows of No. 3
St Eve's discussing the same subject.

"I like the idea of old Coles married to Mrs
Traff', or anyone else," said Brookes, with a
chuckle.

"Oh, I didn't say it would be a good thing
for *her*," responded Orford coolly.

"Here he comes. By Jove! now for the
time to take a rise out of him. How do,
Colonel?" addressing the gossip as he drew
near them.

"Ah, Brookes; how do, Orford? Well, what's
the news?"

"Well, the latest is, Colonel," said Brookes, in
a grave voice, "that a man might do worse than
marry Mrs Traff'."

"That certainly is so," said the gossip, with

decision. "In my opinion, she's the cleverest little woman in Christendom."

"So Orford here seems to think," nudging his grinning comrade's elbow; and he has pitched upon *you*, Colonel, as a very tidy, likely sort of spouse for that same clever little woman. Now what do *you* think about it, eh?"

The gossip's beaming and rubicund old face relaxed, fell, and the jaw dropped: in fact, he looked up with what is commonly called "a face as long as a fiddle."

"*I!*" he exclaimed incredulously, "*I* marry Mrs Traff'! MRS TRAFF', *I!*" and then he added an ejaculation which unmistakably came from the very bottom of his heart, "*Good* GOD!"

Marcus Orford burst out laughing.

"Well, ta-ta, Colonel, you'd better think it over; you might do worse, you know."

"Yes, I might," returned Colonel Coles, with feeling. "I might go and drown myself," and then he went on his way, no longer jubilant and beaming, but a sadder, if not a wiser man, suffering still from the effects of the shock, and repeating, "I—I marry Mrs Traff'! Good GOD!"

"You took the wind out of his sails, Lester," said Orford, with a laugh.

"Yes, I fancy I did rather. I thought he was going to have a fit on the spot. Poor old chap; but that would be an ending for him; why, a sharp little woman like that would turn him inside out in next to no time. By Jove! but

wouldn't she dust his jacket for him every now
and again," and then, the picture of the little
widow a-dusting the old Colonel's capacious
jacket being too much for further speech, Lester
Brookes went off in the direction which his
Colonel had taken, with a happy air of hilarity,
as if something particularly pleasant had just
happened to him.

Left to himself, Marcus Orford walked slowly
in the opposite direction, turned the corner to
the right, went at a moderate pace along Cardella Street in the direction of the club; then,
apparently with not a small amount of sudden
decision, turned sharply in at the gate of the
Winter Garden, not at all as if he had had any
intention of doing so, but exactly as if the idea
that the Winter Garden was there, and might as
well be walked into, had but just presented itself
to him.   And when he got there, he found what
he had often so found of late, a young lady
sitting under a large mulberry tree—a young
lady with a book in her hand, whose name was
Madge Trafford.   And oh, how his heart went
pit-a-pat, pit-a-pat when he saw her, and she,
looking up from her book, greeted him with a
smile.

"What are you reading?" he asked, as he sat
down.   Yes, they had already got to that, that
he never now asked her if he might sit down
beside her.   "Oh, *The Gate of Paradise.*   How
do you like it?"

"Immensely : it's a charming book."

"Yes, and he—er, Tempest, that is, Murphy, is such a good fellow. I'm sure you would like him awfully."

"Yes, I think I should," she answered.

"He's on leave now with a broken leg, but I believe he rejoins next week sometime. I will introduce him to you if I may."

"Oh, yes, I should like it very much; but I am going away on the 16th."

"Yes, your aunt told me you were going away," he said; "I have just come from your house. I've been asking her to bring you and your cousins to the regimental sports on the 17th; our sports, you know; and she told me you were going away."

"Yes, I am going on the 16th," in a tone of regret.

"You would have liked it?" eagerly catching at her tone.

"Yes, I should have liked it," looking at him with her great, frank, handsome eyes.

"Don't you think you could stay for it?" he asked, more eagerly still. "It would only make two days' difference to your friends, and it would be such a pleasure to me to entertain you in my rooms. Don't you think you could put off your visit, just for two days?"

For one moment the girl's face lighted up with intense pleasure; then the memory of a morning a week or two back, when Mrs Traff'

had not been in the best of tempers, came to her,
bringing with it a recollection of one or two
scathing, stinging remarks commenting upon
the foolishness of her "attempting to attract
the Honourable Marcus Orford's notice"; the
bright, pleased light faded out of her eyes, and
the lovely flush which his pleading words had
brought into her cheeks died away.

"No, I could not come," she said, shaking her
head sadly; "do not ask me, I must go to Amshurst on the 16th."

"Your friends will not—"

"It is nothing to do with my friends," she
interrupted; "I would rather not put off going
to them."

"Is it," he asked very gently, "that *you*
would rather no' come to *my* rooms?"

"Oh, no,' not at all—not at all," nervously,
"it—it is quite for another reason."

Some glimmer of the truth crept into Orford's
brain.

"I think I understand," he said slowly; "ah,
well, never mind, the time will come; if it is not
you, it will all come right by-and-by."

SIDELIGHT.

MRS FAIRLIE.

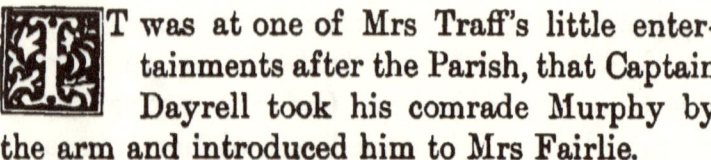IT was at one of Mrs Traff's little entertainments after the Parish, that Captain Dayrell took his comrade Murphy by the arm and introduced him to Mrs Fairlie.

"This is the man who wrote *The Gate of Paradise*, you know," he added.

Mrs Fairlie entered into the subject with ravenous interest, and at once conversation slipped into full swing, for it happened that the author was particularly sore just then about a little difference he had had with his publishers, and rejoiced to find a new and intelligent listener.

"You know they wanted the story lengthened," he said, settling himself for a good long comfortable, cosy talk — "so I wrote *all* that chapter on the Married Woman's Property Act, you know."

"Yes," said Mrs Fairlie, with intense interest. She did not happen to have read the book, but he was a fine good-looking fellow, so she dissembled a little. "Well?"

"And I never thought of asking for a penny, not for a penny. And then afterwards, when the seventh edition came out, and I wanted some copies, they sent me a bill,—a bill, if you'll believe me."

"Never heard of such a thing—such a book—such— Oh! how do you do, Mr Orford? we are talking about *The Gate of Paradise*."

"Ah! yes; good book, isn't it? By-the-bye, have you read it?" asked Orford? and Mrs Fairlie was so utterly taken aback by the point-blank question, that she stammered,—

"No-o. I—er—haven't," though she could have bitten her tongue off afterwards for having been so honest.

"Oh! Captain Orford," she said reproachfully, when the author had taken himself away in disgust, "how could you—a man of the world —ask me such a foolish question? Everybody knows one has not to *read* a book to be able to talk about it, and Captain Murphy seemed to take it so for granted that I *had* read it—and, really, you have made it very embarrassing for me, you have indeed."

"Never mind, Mrs Fairlie," Orford laughed. "I'm awfully sorry, of course; but, remember, you can say with Washington, '*Father, I cannot tell a lie.*'"

"There's some comfort in that," said Mrs Fairlie, in a distinctly mollified tone.

CHAPTER XVI.

"MR WINKS."

GEOFFRY WILLIAM DELACOURT, LORD CHARTERHOUSE, was perhaps the prettiest specimen of a bold dragoon who was to be found in the whole of the service; and when I say pretty, I really mean pretty! He was a lovely boy! He would have made a lovely girl, and, as a matter of fact, very often had assumed the garb and manner of the fair sex when taking part in dramatic representations at school and 'varsity. He was a slight, slim person, under the middle height, with a fine pink-and-white complexion which rivalled even that of the fair Polly. Added to this he had yellow hair, the real English flaxen shade, and a pair of grey-blue eyes, with a serene and seraphic expression like a dove or a little child.

At Delacourt there were several portraits of

him as a little lad taken in all the beauty of
gay-coloured velvet and point-lace; but the last,
in his gold-broidered uniform, outshone them all,
though the round young face, with its serene
mouth and straight, seraphic gaze, was more like
that of a girl than a man of war.

In the regiment he was generally called "Mr
Winks," varied occasionally by "Winks," and,
as a grudging compliment to his personal appearance, "Madame Rachel." Perhaps, if he
had been in the Guards, he would have rejoiced in some one or other of the pretty names
which, according to certain ladies of the pen,
are invariably bestowed upon officers of those
regiments by one another, he might have been
called "The Cherub," or "The Seraph," or
"Adonis," or "Beauty Charterhouse," or even,
by a very, very long stretch of the imagination into the realms of slanginess and mascu-
linity, "Pretty Face"! But then, of course, he
was not a Guardsman, only a Dragoon, therefore he had to put up with regimental names
no more attractive than "Mr Winks" for every-
day use and "Madame Rachel" for high days
and holidays.

Now Mr Winks, though he was small and
slender and pretty, was not shy, nor yet over
and above sensitive. He had, moreover, the
courage of his opinions, and as it suited him
in mind, body, and estate to be a distinctly
and undeniably good young man, he was good

accordingly. By good I do not mean goody-goody. I do not mean that he walked about the barrack square with a Bible in one hand and a bundle of pious leaflets in the other—not a bit of it; or that he held prayer-meetings in the troop-rooms, and made a practice of saying a word in season as he went the round of the dinners, or that he ever endeavoured to touch men's hearts while under the softening influence of pack-drill.

No; Mr Winks never did any of these things, and yet in the Black Horse he had the same character that he had had from the days of velvet suits and point-lace collars; the best of all characters in my estimation, that of being a straight-going, steady chap, whom nothing would turn from a line which he conceived to be his duty. If Mr Winks had once announced that he could not afford a certain extravagance, the officers of the Black Horse knew perfectly well that no persuasions of theirs or any one else's would induce him to change the fiat; if Mr Winks once said that a certain line of conduct was not right—"shady" was generally his way of describing behaviour which others might and usually did call by a much harder term—it very soon became well known that no power upon earth could make him say or think any differently.

Consequently, being this sort of young gentleman, when Mr Winks wanted to invite some

ladies to tea on the occasion of the regimental
sports, he—not being able to ask them to admire the fine and enlightening view of back
yards which the windows of his quarters, situ-
ated at the back of Orford's, commanded—had
not the smallest hesitation in going boldly into
the ante-room, and saying,—

"Will any of you fellows lend me a front
room for the sports? I want to have some
ladies to tea."

"Sweet youth," ejaculated Orford, "I also am
going to have ladies to tea."

"Therefore, I pray thee, have me excused,"
quoted Mr Winks flippantly.

"Yes, exactly. Now there's Dayrell—"

"Awfully sorry," said Dayrell, "but the Lord
Bishop is going to honour me. Otherwise—"

"I have married a wife, and therefore I cannot come," laughed Mr Winks.

"Married a wife," repeated Dayrell. "Well,
I daresay I shall some day, but, believe me, it
won't be out of Blankhampton Palace when I do
that."

"You can have my rooms, Winks," said Staunton. "I'm not going to ask any company."

"Oh! thanks, awfully," returned Mr Winks,
in a very grateful tone. "You're a real good
fellow, Staunton. I'll do as much for you some
day."

"Thanks. By-the-bye, who's going to entertain Lady Mainwaring?"

" Not I," cried one. " Nor I," added another. " Nor I," denied a third.

" Has anyone asked her, I wonder?" said Staunton.

" Oh! my dear chap," rejoined Orford, " don't worry yourself about her ladyship; she'll ask herself, never fear."

" She has," came in a very small voice from behind a newspaper.

" What! *already?*" cried Orford. " Well, 'pon my word, my little bit of information to Lady Mainwaring has been seed not sown on stony ground! I saw she was impressed by the few details I gave her of young Pitch-and-Toss's private affairs, but I'd no idea she would act upon it so sharply."

" Well, it was quite by a fluke that I was so honoured," Brookes explained, with a very modest air. " The fact is, I happened to be standing by the Colonel at the Mayoress's afternoon reception the other day, and Lady Mainwaring came up to us and said, ' My *dear* Colonel Urquhart, *how* are you?'

" The Colonel said that he was very well, and trusted her ladyship was the same. Whereupon her ladyship returned in a plaintive tone that she was as well as could be expected; and, by-the-bye," Lester Brookes added reflectively, " I always thought that was the sort of answer given at a door when one goes to make inquiries? However, the Colonel didn't ask her

N

to explain herself further, which I think rather nettled her; anyhow, she informed him in a very pointed and acid manner that he was looking better than she had at all thought to see him.

"'How is that?' asked the Colonel, apparently not seeing the drift of her observation, though every one else did who was standing near.

"'I thought you'd be more—more—er—er—' began her ladyship with ghastly gaiety.

"The Colonel put his head on one side and waited There was a long pause. The Colonel changed the position of his head and put it on the other side, and then he said—'Ye—s?' in an inquiring tone. Lady Mainwaring looked like an eel in a frying-pan, or most of anything perhaps like a cat on hot bricks.

"'You were saying?' said the chief, after another awful pause. And then her ladyship gave a last wriggle, squirmed right round, you know, and tried to laugh it off.

"'Oh! nothing, nothing, only my fun, you know. And er—er—I hear, Colonel Urquhart, that your regimental sports are coming off soon. I hope you are going to ask *us?*'"

"Yes. I told you so!" broke in Orford. But, lor! fancy *her* having a shot at the Colonel."

"What did the Colonel say?" inquired Staunton.

"Oh! he bowed, said he should have been

charmed, er—delighted, and all the rest of it,
but unfortunately Lady Hamilton had asked
him for his rooms, and was going to bring a
large party. Upon which her ladyship expressed such bitter disappointment that the Colonel
calmly offered her my room instead, saying, as
it was just above his sitting-room, it would have
a better view of the sports.

"So what could I do but grin and look as pleased
as I knew how, and tell a lot of lies expressive of
joy, which no power upon earth could make me
feel ? And the old cat gushed till I was nearly
ill, called me *dear* Mr Brookes and all the rest
of it ; said it was so *good* of me to ask them—*to
ask them*," he went on, in utter disgust, " when
of my own free will I would have as soon have
asked two tabby-cats and a baa-lamb."

" Which is the baa-lamb ?" asked Staunton,
with interest ; he had heard of Lady Mainwaring
and had seen her nieces.

" That Elizabeth !" from the sold and disgusted Brookes. " However, they're the Colonel's
guests, not mine, and I shall not stop and entertain them ; to that I've made up my mind."

" By-the-bye, who is having Mrs Traff ?"
asked Dayrell, when the laugh at poor young
"Pitch and Toss" had subsided.

" Me!' responded Orford promptly. " Oh !
yes, you fellows may all laugh, but, for my
part, I have a profound respect for Mrs Traff.
By Jove ! she's a downright sensible little

woman ; and besides that, she's more amusing
than nineteen people out of twenty that one
meets."

" Yes, that's so," cried Brookes ; " if it had been
Mrs Traff I should have been glad enough, but
Lady Mainwaring, oh, lor !"

A laugh followed this, and then Staunton
suddenly asked who Mr Winks was going to
have ?

" Can't say, I'm sure," returned Austin, " but
I should think the stout old lady with the
pretty daughter ; Mr Winks seems awfully gone
in that quarter."

" Gone ! Poor Winks," laughed Orford. " By-
the-bye, if she was the girl who was engaged to
Eliot Cardella, how is it that she is Miss Antrobus
still ? I think, indeed I'm quite sure, that Eliot
told me in one of his letters she had married
some Jew fellow."

" Ah ! no, no ; Eliot's information was a little
premature," struck in Colonel Coles. " I remember the circumstances perfectly."

" Yes, trust you to do that, Colonel," laughed
Orford. " Well, how was it premature ? "

" This way, I believe there is a sort of bogie
lover in the background, some fellow who admires
Polly, and—and hasn't exactly come up to the
scratch yet. But the old lady keeps him always
to the front as a sort of bogie to frighten other
fellows with A sort of 'If-you-don't-make-haste-
and-secure-the-prize-this-applicant-will.' See?"

"Yes, yes, exactly; but that game won't do at all with Mr Winks," said Orford. "I see I must put her up to a straight tip, as I did her ladyship. Well, I'm off into the town. Where am I going? Well, if you must know, I'm going to have tea at the Mansion House. Yes, awful joke. By-by. Oh, is that you Lester? You going to worship at the civic shrine?"

"Yes; I thought I might as well; they always have such pretty girls at the Mansion House, and they're fresh too. I mean, one doesn't meet them everywhere else. It's rather a bore meeting the same girls over and over again; they get to know one so awfully well, and, somehow, one would as soon know them a little less, don't you think?"

"A very great deal less," returned Orford, with a laugh. "It always seems to me, in a place like this, if you don't want to think seriously of marrying, that it is best to make fast friends with the young married women."

"There's Mrs Fairlie," broke in Brookes doubtfully, "but somehow I don't quite think I should care about knowing very much of Mrs Fairlie. She's so awfully intimate with old Coles, goes for long country walks with him, I'm told, and generally makes herself and him rather look idiotic. Of course, you know old Coles is all very well, good fellow and all that, I daresay, but somehow I don't seem quite to care about a woman who *flirts* with him. And besides, she laughs

up her face, and I always hate that in anybody."

Marcus Orford laughed all over his.

" Up her face," he repeated, in a puzzled tone.
" What do you mean ? "

" I mean, well, er—up her face, you know."

" But I don't know," Orford insisted.

" Well—er—the corners of her mouth go right
up when she laughs. I—I may be prejudiced,
but it always seems to me to give a wolfish sort
of look to a face. I daresay she can't help it,
but it always makes me think of snakes and
such-like."

" Ah ! yes, yes ; I see. Well, I don't particularly admire Mrs Fairlie myself; still, she's
quite good enough for him. It's odd, but I've
thought myself two or three times how like a
snake she is. Don't like snakes myself. I remember once out in Australia—yes, I was out
as a boy with my tutor. Why ? Oh ! my lungs
got a trifle out of order, and the doctors sent
me out there to rough it for a year. I don't
suppose," Orford said, with a laugh, " that I
ever had the faintest notion of what roughing
it really is, for we had plenty of money and
well-supplied kits : but still, it was a much
rougher life than I had been used to, and regularly made a man of me. Well, I remember we
once were right up country, on a bit of a tour
into the interior. We hadn't seen a single soul
all day, and made our camp under a big tree.

We soon got a roaring fire alight, and, after we had hobbled our horses to prevent them straying too far, set about getting our tea ready. We had bread and meat and cake, and, of course, the tea was soon made in the genuine Australian fashion. What's that? Well, in a 'billy,' of course, otherwise a good-sized tin pan like a paint-pot. You get your water boiling in this, and just at boiling point drop your tea in and snatch the "billy" off the fire at once. Yes, you get perfect tea that way, perfect.

"Well, we got our tea, and as Australian nights are frightfully hot at that time of the year, undressed and crept into our blankets; or rather we did not do that, for we sat talking over the fire and chucking stones at the blessed opossums as they squatted in the trees overhead, wondering when we were going off to sleep, that they might get at the provision bag. There are heaps of snakes out there, you know. Oh, yes, heaps; rattle-snakes and black-snakes, and—and—hoop snakes."

"What are they?" Brookes asked.

"Oh, well, they're rather a queer sort of snake; they stick their tales into their mouths and make a hoop of themselves, and, by Jove! they go trundling about the country at a deuce of a rate, I can tell you."

There was a moment's pause.

"I don't believe that," said Brookes, a little

puzzled by the other's apparently truthful air.

Marcus Orford burst out laughing.

"No; but really there are rattlesnakes and black snakes out there by the dozens. On this particular night, when I crept in between the folds of the blankets, I felt something as cold as ice against my bare leg. I jumped up and gave a sort of shudder—ugh—gh—gh. 'That's a snake,' I thought, and shouted for Mortimer, my tutor; and sure enough a minute later out there glided a great black snake about six feet long, which had been attracted by our big fire. Mortimer didn't waste a minute, but snatched a blazing log of wood out of the fire and took a shot with it at him, breaking his back. Another black joker, bigger and longer than the first, came out then, and we went after him, leaving the disabled one wriggling about in a fine stew. However, the second visitor got away, so we came back and finished off number one, and hung it up afterwards by the tail to a tree, with a piece of paper round its neck—

"'Killed by Hugh Mortimer and Marcus Orford,' with the date.

It was an long time, a very long time, before either of us felt inclined to turn in again, till at last weariness got too much for us, and we had to make up our minds to be very brave and chance it. It was a deuce of a time before I dropped asleep. But that was the only night that we were ever in the least uncomfortable."

"You had a very narrow shave on the whole."

"As narrow as could be, without being bitten. It would have been all up with me then. Yes, it was a most unpleasant sensation to feel that icy wriggle along one's leg—horrid! And, 'pon my word, Mrs Fairlie gives one pretty much the same shudder all over. Well, here we are. Now, go and do your best to bring old John out like a stone out of a catapult."

SIDELIGHT.

MRS JOHN DOUGHTY.

AS all the world knew, young John Doughty had made a very good marriage, but then, as all the world thought and said, young Mrs John Doughty had decidedly married beneath her. For old John was a plasterer, and not a particularly honest one at that; indeed, dark tales went about among Blankhampton folk—*folk*, not in society—of a will, and an inability of old John to stop in a room by himself.

It was, perhaps, for this reason that it behoved young Mrs John to be as haughty as if she had been born of the blood-royal. Anyway, one day at Mrs Traff's she chanced to be talking to a young gentleman of the Blankshire Regiment, who had just come back to headquarters after a spell of service at Westbury, one of the biggest manufacturing towns in the county.

"Horrid place," she said. "My sister lives there, and hates it."

"Yes? Ah! of course I wasn't there long enough really to know what sort of place it was," he answered.

"Oh! horrid place; no so-ci-atay whatever."

"Is that so? But who lives in those big houses up the West End?"

"Oh! foreigners and manufacturing people. There is no soci-atay *whatever*."

Oh! society—society—society! *What* a game it is! Young John's father was a plasterer, and *his* father wheeled a barrow all the days of his life, while·young John goes to a calico ball as *his* father, who was—God knows what!

CHAPTER XVII.

"*PLANTY-LA.*"

MR LESTER BROOKES obeyed the last instruction so well that the grandly-gilded door was flung open as if by an electric shock, and a little old man appeared on the large mat, with its friendly "Salve!" within. He was a lovely old man, with large, mild blue eyes, and a very benign expression upon his roseate old face; his nose was large and aquiline, his whiskers and hair were snow-white, the first more abundant than the last, which revealed a smooth and shining pink pate. He wore a modified kind of Court suit, consisting of black knee-breeches and silk stockings, with low shoes and plain silver buckles: above this plain evening clothes, and his shirt had a frill to it. And this little old man was the good fairy who watched over the fortunes of the Mayors of Blankhampton,—that is to say, their social fortunes,—who guided, with the strong firm hand of one who knows his path and has trodden it many a time, the often faltering footsteps of the Sir Thomases and Georges and Johns who sat in the post of honour on the aldermanic and magisterial bench.

And it was said in Blankhampton that he ruled them with a rod of iron! Small wonder that it was so, for he knew so much of forms and ceremonies, they so little; he was so thoroughly at home among the pomp and vanities which appertain unto places of honour, they were so painfully new-fangled and *gauche;* they were flurried and anxious, like Martha of old careful and troubled about many things; he was invariably as cool as a cucumber—and not so green. Oh, he was a wonderful man, old Martin, and a great power in Blankhampton society. He knew everybody, and everybody knew him. He was steeped to the very eyes in the lore and genealogy of the place; he could tell you all the history for many and many a generation of the heads of society, which, if you were a stranger in the town, was almost enough to set your hair on end for ever, like the hair of the beautiful Circassian lady who went about some years ago in company with the Siamese twins and Miss Anna Swann. He could tell you how Doughty the lawyer (who married the late Bishop's daughter, when he was archdeacon of Idleminster) was the son of his

dear old friend John Doughty, the plasterer;
and he would add, with what was apparently an utter absence of satire, that
"Young John goes all round about now;
came 'ere the other day to a calico ball
dressed as 'my great-grandfather.' True, I
can't say what his *great*-grandfather was, but
I minded his grandfather very well when I
was a lad — he lived up a passage on Toft
Hill, and wheeled a plasterer's barrow all the
days of his life. Oh, yes, what I remembers
the Doughtys well enough—of course I do—
root *and* branch. And there was another
of them girls"— meaning the daughters of
the late bishop — "she married old Dollin's
lad, the third one! Ah, *'is* father was a
breeches maker. Oh, yes, I mind all the lot
of 'em. The young ladies come here and
they shake out their skirts in the 'all and
they smiles at me and says 'Good afternoon,
Martin,' or 'Are you very well, Martin?' and
such like; but perhaps if they knew that I
know so much about their forebears they'd
scarcely be quite so civil. Now there was
two ladies 'ere one day," old Martin said to
me in a tone of confidence, after, for a con-
sideration in small change, showing me over
the state rooms of the Mansion House, "who
had come to call on 'My Lady.' One was a
homely old body without any sham about her,
as rich as Crœsus, though they say her hus-

band kept her that tight in 'is time that she
never thought they were worth more than
an old song, so to speak. Eh, dear, dear; but
it was funny. She's been upstairs sitting with
My Lady, and passing through this very 'all
she meets with Mrs Monson, who is wife of
one of the clergymen at the Parish.

"' Oh ! 'ow d'you do, Mrs Partingdon ?' says
Mrs Monson, 'I haven't been to see you for—
AGES ! I am very remiss, but really I've so
many calls to make.'

"' I only came back last week,' returned Mrs
Partingdon.

"' Oh, *dear*, 'ave you been away ?' says Mrs
Monson.

"' Yes, I've been away nine months,' answers
Mrs Partingdon civilly. 'But I was obliged to
come back and take a peep at the old place.
It's dull, but I'm fond of it.'

"' And so am I,' says the other.

"' I daresay, I'm a real Blankshire woman—'

"' And *I*,' says Mrs Monson, with a sweet
smile, 'I am of Blankshire *extraction* too !'

"' Blankshire ex-tract-ion !' cries the old lady,
with a regular snort. 'Blank-shire ex-tract-
ion, Mrs Monson ! Why, dear me, yes, what
we all know ! Of course you are, when your
grandfather kept a chemist's shop in Bonner
Street, and your Uncle Philip too. What, dear
me, I've been in your Uncle Philip's shop dozens
of times. Blankshire *ex—traction !* '

"'Oh, I think you are mistaking me for some distant cousins of mine,' began Mrs Monson, when the old lady cut her short.

"'Oh, dear no, Mrs Monson; you're one of William Garforth's daughters. What, dear me, I'm like to know. Why, your father and all his brothers and sisters and *me* played children together. Blankshire *extraction* indeed ! What, I'm like to know.'"

That was only one of the many odd stories stored up in old Martin's memory. There was one about the father of two very prominent families in Blankhampton society at the present day; one Anthony Brown, the father of Richard and John, respectively the husbands of Mrs Richard (more familiarly known as Mrs Dick) and Mrs John. "Ah, dear, dear," old Martin began, "but Mrs Dick's a pretty woman, one of a pretty-looking family. I think there was seven of 'em—all pretty almost. You know I hear a good deal of what the different gentlemen says. Lord, no, they never minds me. There was seven of them Preston girls; and the gentlemen up to the Barricks a year or two back used to call 'em 'Sweet Spirits.' Yes, it might have had something to do with the father being in that line. I can't say. Mrs Dick's about the prettiest of all the lot, and Mrs John, she's what they call a fine woman. Well, old Anthony Brown—bless me, I remember him ever since I was a lad—he was bad in his legs; anyhow, he didn't walk for many and many a year before he was took, and I remember one evening, a week or two after his death, I met the old lady out just round the corner by St Eve's. 'Good evening, Mr Martin,' says she. So I just stopped, and I says, 'I was very sorry, ma'am, to hear of your loss, very sorry,' and then I adds something about it's being a blessed release after so much suffering, when the old lady caught me up as quick as lightning. 'A blessed release, Mr Martin,' says she. 'Ay, you may well say that; it's been more like living with a fiend than aught else for the last twenty years; blessed release indeed,' and then she bounces on, leaving me what my present lady calls '*planty-la*'!'"

And this was the lovely old man who flung open the door, and stood bowing and smiling a welcome to Orford and Brookes.

"My lady at home?" said Orford. He and Martin were great friends.

"Yes, sir. Walk in, gentlemen," Martin responded.

"Many people upstairs?" Orford asked.

"A goodish few, sir," said the old man, as he passed in front of them to conduct them up the grand staircase.

And sure enough, when they found themselves in the state-room, they were in the midst of a large assembly of well-dressed people, mostly ladies. There was "dear Lady Mar-

garet," a handsome, fresh - coloured buxom
woman, with a blue feather in her bonnet,
and a new fur flounce on her sealskin coat,
which was much noticed and remarked upon.
And there was a little pink-cheeked parson,
with a short allowance of nose, who was paying
her great attention. And there was "the dear
Dean," the most commanding figure in all the
room, standing firm and true upon his handsome
feet and legs, deep in a discussion as to the
respective merits of Epps's or Fry's cocoa for
the use of the Hospital. And there was Colonel
Coles, with his beaming and rubicund old countenance shining with delight as he retailed the
very last tit-bit of gossip to a select audience
in one corner; it was a very sweet morsel, no
less than the first news of a marriage between
one of the Antrobus family and the pretty
bright-eyed widow at the other end of the
room, with a bunch of white flowers on her
black bonnet such as showed she was getting
over her loss; there was about as much truth
in the story as if they had said she was going
to marry the Dean, notwithstanding the presence of the handsome lady in the sealskin coat
and blue feather. And there was Mrs Hugh
Antrobus, beaming as broadly as the old gossip
himself, who had folded her fat arms across
her capacious person, and blandly shut her
eyes to the fact that Lord Charterhouse was
bending very closely over the fair Polly's chair;

and the fair Polly was looking very lovely,
but, at the same time, somewhat as if under
all the laces and frills and loops of ribbon which
adorned her person, diligent search might dis-
cover " a button short." And in another corner
there sat a wonderful lady, larger and more
blooming even than Mrs Hugh, who smiled more
broadly, and every now and again smoothed
down her rich gown with a proud and well-
satisfied gesture ; the young lady beside her was
speaking of it.

" Why, Lady Newton," she exclaimed, " I
thought you never wore a dress that cost less
than a hundred pounds!"

" Lor'! my dear," cried Lady Newton, in a rich
and oily voice that spoke volumes of turtle soup
and such-like fattening dainties.

"That's what they say," persisted the girl, with
sparkling eyes.

" Lor', my dear, you surely never believe all
them tales!" Lady Newton returned, with a
good-natured contempt of Blankhampton tittle-
tattle, which was what it richly deserved. " Sir
Stephen *did* go to a long figure when I 'ad my
velvet gown for my at 'ome as Mayoress; but
lor', a 'undred pounds goes a long way in a gown
—a long way. Oh! my dear, you should never
take notice of what you 'ear. Dear no. When
I 'ear Mr So-and-so has had forty thousand
left him, why, I divide it and halve it again,
and then I about get at the truth of it."

Then Marcus Orford's roving grey eyes spied
out Miss Laura Trafford trying very hard to
flirt with the rich young minor canon, Mr
Evelyn Gabrielli, who had put on his most
ascetic and ritualistic air, and was trying his
best to look as if he were giving the young
lady no encouragement; while his great chum
and contemporary, Mr Hooper, had secured the
attention of a very bonny girl, one of the
Leslies, and was making the running as well
as he knew how, which between you and me
was at a good rate.   Eustace Hooper had come
to the town on appointment to the Parish years
before, and had had for some years about the
best time of any man out of barracks.   Clever
fellow—he announced at once that he wanted
to marry as soon as possible, and oh! what a
good time he had after that.   He had as many
invitations and attentions and kindnesses as
Colonel Urquhart and Marcus Orford put together—he was *fêted* far and wide—he was
pretty well eaten alive.

He wanted to marry as soon as possible! and
yet, after eight years had gone by, he was still
fluttering from flower to flower, ostensibly making his choice.   Ah! but Blankhampton mothers
and daughters had got to know him, and Eustace
Hooper found that life had considerably changed
for him since the advent of Evelyn Gabrielli—
he had to make all the running now.   Bless me,
how odd it all was!   As for Gabrielli, there was

no deception about him: at once he announced
his firm belief in the advisability of the celibacy
of the clergy—with the same result exactly as
attended Eustace Hooper's declaration that he
wanted to marry and settle !

Miss Laura, Mrs Traff's youngest flower, having got a little tired of officers—she said they
were really so frivolous, she liked a man to have
some serious views of life—had become possessed
of an idea that to be Mrs Gabrielli would suit
her very well. He was young, he was rich, he
was a good size, and most people thought handsome, and he had the finest collection of rings
she had ever seen owned by any one man. Altogether there were nineteen of them—nineteen
rings, pearls and diamonds, sapphires, rubies, tur-
quoise, and pale pink coral, ornaments fit for a
princess or for the dainty white and tiny hands
of Mr Evelyn Gabrielli. Marcus Orford caught
with an inward laugh the look of positive fright
upon his face, and just then noticed that Mrs
Traff' was sitting on a circular ottoman almost
in the centre of the large room; her back was
turned to him, but she was speaking to a lady
beside her so that her rather remarkable profile
was well presented for his inspection. What the
lady was saying he could not hear, but a moment
later, in a pause of the babel of voices which
filled the air, a fragment of Mrs Traff's reply
was wafted to him.

" Oh, yes, but not until after Madge's marriage."

SIDELIGHT.

OLD MARTIN.

"AND there'll be old Martin," said one
speaker.

"Oh!" returned the other, doubtfully, "but I thought when we went into the
Mansion House we could do without old Martin
—you see we've got our own butler."

"Do without Martin!" cried the first. "Oh!
my dear fellow, impossible. He's part of the
ceremony."

"Well, if you think so—"

"If I think so! I tell you, you *can't* do without Martin."

"Very well," with a resigned sigh, and so it
ended.

"But," said the first man to himself an hour
later, "what the devil did he want to do without
Martin for?"

. . . .

"Yes, my lady, certainly, my lady. I will

attend to it, your ladyship," said old Martin, in his courtliest tones, as he shut the carriage door.

"I do detest that Martin," said my lady in a burst of feeling; "he's so obsequious."

.   .   .   .

"How old Martin does palaver Lady Smith," remarked one leader of Blankhampton society to another. "Have you ever noticed it? He is always very profuse with his use of their titles, but it seems to me that Lady Smith gets an extra amount of that kind of attention."

"Yes, and I don't think she much likes it. She regularly *wriggles* under it, poor soul," answered the other with a laugh.

"I suppose she has offended him, and he is paying her out," said the first speaker.

.   .   .   .

Offended him? Not a bit of it—but he was her uncle by marriage, that was all!

CHAPTER XVIII.

L'AMAZONE.

LONG afterwards when Marcus Orford spoke of his sensations as that fragment of conversation fell upon his ears, he declared that never to his dying day, not even if he should live to be a thousand, could he forget the sharp pang of agony which shot through his heart; it caught his breath; it made his brain reel and his eyes grow dim with such a mist as had not clouded their brave grey depths for many and many a year,—in that one moment he realised all that the girl was to him.

"Not until after Madge's marriage!" Words spoken carelessly and without thought, and—he would stake his very life upon it—uttered without the faintest idea that to him they had the sound of a death-knell.

"Not until after Madge's marriage!" Madge's marriage! Madge's marriage! Madge's mar-

riage! Good God! how the two words beat
themselves into his brain! Was he losing his
senses? Was he going to do something stupid
that his head began to rock, and the two words
changed to a loud persistent sound like the
clanging of a large bell? And then he woke
up to find Lester Brookes jogging at his arm,
and the strains of *L'Amazone* waltz, played
by the band of the Rifle corps in the courtyard
below stealing with their subtle and dreamy
delirious beauty through the heated air of the
crowded room; and somehow or other the
fateful words which had just fallen from Mrs
Trafford's lips had set themselves to the music
and came dancing over the hum and chatter
of all those careless voices with a smooth and
graceful swing and rhythm maddening to
him :*—

Un - til aft - er Madge's mar - riage.

Over and over and over again the strains
stole to him from the courtyard, and as many
times did Mrs Trafford's words rise in his
heart and set themselves to the music, "Until
after Madge's marriage."

---

* *L'Amazone* Waltz, by Mrs Vaughan Williams. London:
Hutchings & Romer.

"I say, old chap," said Brookes anxiously, "we'd better get out of this; this hot room is too much for you."

Orford made no demur, and Brookes still keeping hold of his arm got him out of the crowd and down the broad stairs into the hall. There old Martin met them and saw that something was wrong.

"Is anything the matter, gentlemen?" he asked.

"The room upstairs has been a little too much for Captain Orford, Martin," Brookes answered; "it is fearfully hot—fearfully."

"Oh! come into the dining-room, sir, and have a little brandy," Martin urged, with an air of anxious hospitality which was admirable.

So the two officers followed the lovely pink-and-white old man into the great dining-room with its huge silver flagons and tankards and old brass shields; and there, under the influence of the civic O. D. V. Orford came back to his proper senses.

"No, I won't go back again; thanks, Martin," he said in answer to the old man's entreaty that "my lady" would be terribly disappointed with him. "Oh, my lady will get on very well without me; and I don't think I could stand that suffocating room again. But all the same, Lester, don't let me keep you any longer; you go back and I'll take a cab home and lie down. Pray go back, there's a good chap."

"I'll see you int the cab," said Brookes, who was a little scared by the whiteness of Orford's face and lips; then, after a minute or two, when Orford had hailed and entered a cab, and had shut the door, he put his head in at the window and said anxiously, "You're sure you'll be all right, old fellow?"

"Oh! dear, yes; don't waste any more time. I saw Lady Mainwaring on the look-out, and the fair Elizabeth all in full sail hiding a nice comfortable bit of lounge with her skirts. Go back again;" and with a wave of the hand he signified that he was ready to go on.

But although the cab moved off and went at a jog-trot down the street, Lester Brookes did not immediately go back into the Mansion House; on the contrary, he stood and watched the receding vehicle with an anxious and puzzled look upon his well-favoured face.

"I wonder if he overdid it when he was training for those last steeplechases?" he said to himself. "I don't like that ashen grey look on a man's face; it generally shows there is *something* seriously wrong—don't like all those Turkish baths myself,—beastly things; they always seem to play the very devil with the constitution. I wonder if poor old Orford's heart has got out of order?" which was just the true state of the case, though not quite in the way that Mr Lester Brookes meant.

However, he went back to the big room,

and after a time found himself drifted into
Elizabeth Damerel's way; he found too that
Marcus Orford had not been speaking at
random when he said she was hiding a nice
comfortable bit of the lounge upon which
she was sitting with her skirts, but—there
are none so blind as those who won't see,
and Lester Brookes acted upon the saying—
he did not avail himself of her thoughtful
care for his comfort and welfare. He stood
and talked to her for a few minutes, but,
though he had to bend down very much (for
he was a big fellow), and she had to crane
her neck up still more, and even then did
not hear everything he said, he did not sit
down upon the velvet-covered seat beside her,
not even though she drew her skirt aside with
a gesture which was significance itself, and
went so far as to give the velvet cushion several
inviting little pats with her large and plump,
well-gloved hand.

But oh! for the perversity of mankind—
he did not greatly admire Miss Elizabeth
Damerel, and he had never wholly forgiven
Lady Mainwaring for wishing, after picking
him up and dropping him like a red-hot cinder,
to take him up again and "put him in her
pocket." So, as in the case of a horse which
one man may lead to the water, where twenty,
ay, and twice twenty, will not be able to make
him drink, he obstinately refused to see the

hidden lounge or the drawing aside of the
pretty autumn costume, or the little encouraging pats of the plump hand, and presently
he went on his way, leaving the fair Elizabeth
what old Martin would have called "planty-la."

He very soon found himself where he felt a
great deal more comfortable and more safe, that
is, beside Mrs Traff, who made much of him, and
asked him if she did not see Captain OR-ford
come into the room with him ? Oh! he was
not well. Oh, dear, she *was* so sorry; what
had he been doing with himself that the mere
heat of the room had upset him so completely ?
Oh, Mr Brookes thought he had been training
too hard for the steeple-chases in the spring.
Really? Oh, dear, she *was* so sorry; and then
she added, that she thought him looking *so* well
only a few days previously. Dear, dear, how
terribly the training must have affected him to
make him so unwell *all* these months afterwards.

And so the good lady wandered on, while, at
the other end of the room, her ladyship was
making stereotyped replies to the remarks with
which everybody greeted her.

"How *very* warm it is, my dear Lady Smith."

"Very 'ot indeed, very 'ot."

"And how is Sir Timothy ?" in an anxious
tone.

"Pretty well, thank you. He was 'ere till a
few minutes ago. He 'ad a meeting to attend."

As a matter of fact, quite an hour and a half
had elapsed since Sir Timothy had slipped away
to attend a meeting, which consisted of smoking
the friendly cigar and drinking the convivial
glass of sherry with a friend at the hotel just
across the street. But her ladyship, in the
flurry of receiving so many visitors — faces
known and unknown, some visitors whom she
was terribly afraid of, and some visitors who
were equally afraid of her—having got firmly
hold of the phrase, stuck to it with a devotion
worthy of a better and more lasting remark.
Poor soul, those same receptions were a bitter
trial to her, as they had been to many a good
and worthy wife and mother before her; and
really, when you come to consider the matter,
to consider that for a whole afternoon she has
to sit up in a corner almost by herself, arrayed
in a gorgeous velvet robe decked with lace and
jewels, with a heavy chain of office weighing
down her shoulders, and a pair of spotless white
kid gloves upon her hands, feeling as any woman
on earth must do, as stiff as buckram, and alter-
nately as hot as fire and as cold as ice, it is
not surprising. There, on a large sofa in lonely
state she has to sit and face—the town! To
see old Martin come in, advance into the middle
of the room and bawl, "Mis-ter—and Miss-is—
JONES!" And to have the Joneses, and the
Brownes, and the Cardellas, and the Traffords,
and all the *Olla Podrida* which go to make up

"sassiety," pouring in upon her in quick succession, until she gets up and shakes hands, and sinks down upon her couch of state in such a whirl of bewilderment, that she scarcely knows what she is saying, or how she is looking, or whether she is standing on her head or her feet, and is really only conscious of one thing, which is, that she wishes fervently and heartily that she had not put on any rings on her poor aching right hand, or that she could get the tight-fitting ten-button white glove off for a minute, that she might remove them. But no—even as the wish forms itself in her heart, old Martin, with his shining pink face and his bald pate appears once more, walking with his own little official strut, and announces a fresh relay of Smiths, and Greens, and d'Arcys. So she has to get up and begin it all over again, "How very hot it is," "And how is Sir Timothy?" and then to wind up with the time-honoured little joke about "make room for somebody else."

It is always the same—everybody always puts the two questions, and then they make their little joke, and quietly sheer off into the more crowded part of the room, where they drink their chocolate or their sherry, and eat the best biscuit they can pick out of the great silver cake-basket carried by one of old Martin's subordinates, where they talk to their friends, and altogether forget the poor sufferer in all her loneliness by the resplendent fireplace, until by·

and-by you hear, " Yes, I must be going now.
Are you going? Oh, wait for me; I'll just go
and say good-bye;" and then back they come
again, and harry her ladyship up once more.

"Good-bye, dear Lady Smith! Charmed to
have seen you. *Good*-bye;" and so it is all
over.

When the cab containing Marcus Orford
moved away from the official residence of the
Chief Magistrate of Blankhampton, leaving
Lester Brookes standing on the pavement, that
gentleman (Orford) was in a state bordering
on delirium. I do not mean to imply that he
was in any danger of putting a bullet into his
head, or any other part of his body; or that
he was likely to suddenly develop a taste for
acrobatic performances in the street, or any
other little freak of that kind. Nevertheless,
his head was in a whirl and aching; aching,
ay, throbbing and well-nigh bursting, and his
heart so full that it was like to break. Poor
Marcus Orford! In all the years of his sunny
and prosperous life, he had never had such a
blow as this. He had been so sure of her, he
had felt so secure in his wooing, for she had
seemed of so little account in the pretty house
in St Eve's, so little cared for or wanted by
her cousins and their mother, to be nobody, and
to have no place of her own.

He knew that he had been a very long time
about his wooing; he knew that had he fixed

his heart upon either Julia or Laura, he would
have asked the question long, long ago, and in
all probability by this time they would have
been on the point of marriage, if, indeed, the
irrevocable step had not actually been taken.
But Madge Trafford was not a girl to be won
in a day. There was that in her manner which
had kept him back even while it had drawn
him on; she was so sweet and friendly, so un-
feignedly glad to see him always, and yet he
felt whenever he was with her that she must
not only be won, but wooed, ay, and wooed
with care and diligence.

And then to find out that it was all no good,
to find that another had been before him, and
that the desire of his heart belonged to another
man—" some other d—d fellow!" to use his
own words upon the subject,—and would never,
never be anything to him as long as he lived.
Oh! it was hard; it was hard! Nor did he
see how to help himself, or anyway out of the
difficulty. He did not try to reason with himself in his disappointment and pain; but he
felt like some wounded animal, desperate and
wild with misery, and ready to fling himself
here and there, as such things do, and dash
himself to pieces in a blind rage and fury.

And then, when he had bitten his lips, and
torn his glove, and banged his stick upon the
opposite seat of the ricketty old cab, which
was the best kind of hired vehicle that Blank-

hampton possessed, until he had brought out
so much dust therefrom that a violent fit of
sneezing recalled him to himself somewhat, he
cooled down a little, and let his thoughts go
sadly back to the happy time when he had
lived on food raised in the Elysian fields and
had inhabited a castle in the air.

He had fancied she would be so glad to exchange her position of—of dependence in the
house of the widow Traff', for that she would
occupy as his wife, the future Lady Ceespring.
And to think some other fellow—yet stay, *she*
had never spoken of anyone else—*she* had never
seemed even to be thinking of anyone else;
supposing she was engaged to someone she
didn't care very much about; supposing it was
somebody that Mrs Traff' had chosen: nothing
could be more likely! And if that were so,
why, might she not be persuaded to get rid
of his rival and seek happiness with him
instead? He was quite sure, in the flush
of this new hope which had so suddenly
sprung up before him, he was quite sure she
liked him—in her own quiet way she had
undoubtedly given him every sign of it, every
encouragement.

At all events he would not give her up without a struggle; if necessary he would fight the
other fellow, and—and—why, here he was at
barracks, and there was Urquhart just coming
away from his stables   Orford stopped the

cab, and threw the man half-a-crown as he turned away.

"I say, Urquhart," he said hurriedly, "I want to go away on the 16th."

"When did you put in to go?'

"The 18th. But I particularly want—nay, I must go on the 16th. If I can't get leave I shall send in my papers—"

"Oh! you'll be able to get it, of course. I'll see what I can do for you," Urquhart answered. "Is anything the matter? You look very seedy."

"Everything is the matter," said Orford with energy. "Everything." However, he did not stay further to enlighten the Colonel, but passed on with a hasty gesture and word of thanks.

As he hurried on with long swinging strides, Colonel Urquhart turned and looked after him curiously.

"Now, what the devil has gone wrong with the fellow?" he asked himself. "I suppose he has got into some mess—a woman at the bottom of it, of course. I wonder if Mrs Traff' has contrived to hook him for her sweet Laura. I shouldn't be the least surprised—anyone could see what the old woman has been after these past few weeks. I hope that's not it. I do dislike that girl—'pon my word, the mother's ten times more attractive. I really don't know if I wouldn't as soon have married her as anyone else if it hadn't been for those girls." But oh! Thomas Urquhart, commanding officer of the Black Horse, if ever you told "a thumping lie" in all your life, that was one, though you only told it to yourself.

SIDELIGHT.

LESTER BROOKES.

ALTHOUGH he was one of the richest men in the service, or, for the matter of that, perhaps in England, and was good-looking and a very fine fellow into the bargain, Lester Brookes was a young man of very quiet and modest demeanour. So simple and unassuming in manner, indeed, that on one or two rare occasions he met with gentlemen of the "too jolly clever by half" type, who fancied he would be an easy person to take in.

One good man of Blankshire celebrity tried it before the whole of the guests at a crowded night at mess.

"Ah!" he began, in a loud, blatant, healthy voice, "You're a 'Varsity oar, aren't you, Mr Brookes?"

"Yes, I was," Brookes answered.

"Oh, you were! Winning year?"

" Yes."

" Ah ! Well, I'll give you a good tip about rowing—one I wouldn't give to everybody, you know—ha—ha—ha ! If—you—want—to—win —a—boat-race—easy,—you have your boat black-leaded !"

" Oh, black-leaded," repeated Brookes quietly.

" Yes. There is nothing like black-leading for making a boat slip through the water *sharp*."

The Blankshire magnate paused for a roar of laughter from the bystanders which did not come—but it came a moment later when Lester Brookes replied,—

" Oh, yes, there is," he said, in a very every-day sort of tone, " and that's having it thoroughly *well castor-oiled !*"

CHAPTER XIX.

URGENT PRIVATE AFFAIRS.

EANTIME Orford went off as fast as he could go to his own quarters, where he composed a fresh application for leave, one of a truly agonising description; the exact terms were "urgent and most important private affairs;" after which, when he had sent it off he had to sit down, and possess his soul in patience until he should get an answer to it. And it was such a long time, nearly a week! More than once he felt as if it was impossible he could wait at all, and that the only course open to him was to go down to St Eve's, and demand the meaning of Mrs Traff's words which he had overheard at the Mayoress's reception; not only demand an explanation from her, but also an assurance from Madge that she was not engaged to any other fellow; or if she was, that she would never, never marry anyone but her humble and adoring lover, Marcus Orford.

Now, as a matter of fact, this would have been a very wise and rational proceeding, and had he followed it he would have been spared a good deal of anxiety ; however, he had unfortunately become possessed of an idea that Mrs Trafford, so far as Madge was concerned, was his enemy, and, indeed, it was quite astonishing how five words, which had not been spoken to him at all, had caused a complete revulsion of feeling towards her. ' Therefore, instead of going down to St Eve's and " having it out," he fretted and worried and fumed the six days away.

An outsider might have thought that he was having a particularly good time in spite of his restlessness and suspense. On the first he got through an easy morning's work, had a very decent lunch — oh, yes, his appetite, Heaven be praised, remained as well as could be desired, and a very great deal better than might reasonably have been expected through, and in spite of all his troubles—then, after prowling into the Winter Garden in search of his lady-fair, whom he did not find, he prowled away from there to a bazaar in aid of a certain small orphanage in which he knew his Madge was interested, and where he fancied it was not impossible he might find her.

He was quite sure that this was the day for

the opening thereof, but nevertheless he stopped at the door of the concert-rooms, where a row of boards and bills generally gave information of all that was "doing" in the town. Yes, "St Dorothy's Orphanage Bazaar, this and following days. Admission before six o'clock two-and-sixpence." Yes, this was it. So Marcus Orford paid his half-crown, and passed within the barrier into the busy throng of grown-up men and women all playing at "keeping shop." He could not see anything of Madge! But he was not at all disheartened, for, as he knew by wide experience in such matters, a very large portion of a bazaar consists of, and is conducted behind the scenes.

There was the art-gallery in the justice-room—the bazaar took place in the Town Hall—and the amateur concerts in the council-chamber, and the refreshments (consisting of very weak and scalding tea, with a meagre allowance of sugar, and the most poverty-stricken milk you can by any possibility imagine, at sixpence a cup, with frowzy bread-and-butter or slabs of sodden cake at the same price), in a marquee in the courtyard, where the "quality" sat on narrow wooden planks, and insulted their stomachs in the cause of charity, bless their dear hearts. To the worldly and the selfish, it may seem but a poor way of doing it, not at all equal to simply dipping a hand into a pocket and bringing out a guinea or two. But believe me, there is no charity so blessed or so sweet as that which costs something in the doing thereof, or which involves some personal sacrifice; and besides these considerations, the good folk of Blankhampton are possessed by the pardonable weakness of liking to get *some*thing in return for their money!

He got through the bazaar proper as fast as an urgent crowd of ravenous young ladies, all apparently eager for his heart's blood, would permit.

"Captain Orford, you'll put in for this? Only a shilling. I worked this on purpose for you." "Captain Orford, flower for your button-hole? fresh gardenia, only half-a-crown, awfully cheap," and so on, until, garnished by a gardenia and some maidenhair, in the proportion of a very little gardenia to a great deal of maidenhair, and bereft of every farthing he had about him, with the exception of a solitary half-crown, to which he held like grim death, as the talisman which would pass him among the beauties of the art-gallery, and the delights of the concert at 4.30, at which only amateur talent was to be heard; he went on his way in hope. Some people prefer it, amateur music, I mean. I remember a man once, writing to me from India, mentioned this very subject. "We only have amateur music out here," he said, "and, by Jove! it's perfect, simply perfect. All amateur—nothing professional, for they won't have them." And then he added, "*They know better.*"

I suppose "they" meant various good ladies in Anglo-Indian society, who were by way of being musical.

Well, having got rid of the bevy of fair high-way-women who had attacked him as soon as he entered the hall, Marcus Orford made his way into the art-gallery, where he found a young lady in charge, of whom, since she had the biggest nose and the worst manners in Blankhampton, he had a special horror. Not finding Madge there, he made short work of the art-gallery, leaving anything but a pleasant impression behind him with this sole daughter of her father's house.

Next he tried the concert-room, but Madge was not there. He listened patiently through a toy symphony, and heard "Old Simon the Cellarer," very badly sung by a very plain and uninteresting youngish man, who, while he might have been moved by the very best of motives, was not entertaining from Orford's point of view. Besides, he had heard the same song sung, equally badly, no fewer than thirteen times by the same gentleman since his military duties had led him to be quartered in the garrison and doubtless familiarity had in his case, as in many another, bred contempt. And after "Old Simon," Mrs Traff's eldest flower, Julia, sang "Dreaming," for which Orford clapped as loudly as his two strong hands

were able, for she sang well in a voice that was
worth paying a good deal more than a shilling
to hear.

And then the young lady with the nose came
up from her art-gallery, and she sang "When
the heart is young," only nobody took much
notice of her, for her's was but a poor little
pipe at best. And then one of his own
brother officers, no other indeed than Sir
Anthony Staunton, came on to sing what
Orford very well knew was his one comic
song.

Naturally Orford became deeply interested
at once. He saw that Staunton was horribly
nervous, for he shot out his cuffs and dragged
up his collar, and pulled the piano slightly
aside so as to face his audience better. And
then, when he was fairly planted and comfortably facing his audience, he became aware that
Orford was there staring with all his grey
steady eyes, which made him ten times more
flurried and nervous than before.

However, he had no choice but to go on, so,
having no music, he carefully picked out a
couple of chords with the right hand and an
octave with the left, and started with a good
thumping tum tum !

It was a song which begins—

> " Will you walk into my shows, sirs ?
>   I've everything—"

but you know the rest.

Well, he got on very nicely until, in an evil moment, he tried to look at his audience and caught the steady gaze of Orford's grey eyes, and then somehow, though he did his best by the aid of a good deal of " side," to recover himself, he made rather a hash of it.

"I've an eld-ah-ly flah-mingo,
  Who walks up and down the stay-ahs!"

But after this he unfortunately stuck fast. He could not remember his words, so jumped up and said he was " Real-lay awful-lay sorray and—er—would begin ov-ah again," after which he shot out his cuffs once more, and starting at the next verse went right manfully through to the very end, and went off the stage with a graceful bow, followed by the rapturous applause of all the ladies, and the " bravo—bravo" of his brother officer, Marcus Orford.

But there was no Madge! and presently in sheer desperation Orford went and sought out Mrs Traff', whom he found sitting, as it were, in judgment with her pert little nose well in air, her sharp little chin well elevated, and her double gold glasses held some inches in front of her.

"In these sort of places," she was saying in her loud and cracked voice to her neighbour, Mrs Mornington-Brown, who, like Mrs Traff' herself, was a new-comer with two daughters,

to establish, though, unlike Mrs Traff', she had
not been altogether successful in Blankhampton
society, probably because none of them possessed
that power of effective "push" which was so dis-
tinguishing a characteristic of the little widow
and her daughters; "in *these* sort of places, there
are so *many* people one does not know," and
then she caught sight of Orford and said, " Ow,
my *dear Cap*-tain Orford, *how* do you do ? "

Orford put on an air of extreme friendliness
which he was far from feeling, and after a few
polite remarks inquired after her young ladies,
adding that he had just heard Miss Julia sing.

"Yes, they are both here. Laura is somewhere."

" I thought your niece was interested in this
orphanage," he said suggestively.

" Ow, yes, I asshaw you Madge has worked
like a slave for *months.*"

" And is she not here ? "

" Ow, yes," confidently, " I'll tell you, Captain
Orford, *all* about it. She has gone to have a
new dress fitted on, for her visit next week you
know."

" Ah ! yes, yes. I thought she was interested
in the—the concern. She told me something
about St Dorothy."

" Oh ! yes, she will be back presently."

Mrs Trafford's tone was very friendly, not
more so than usual, yet, Marcus Orford's sus-
picions having been once aroused, it seemed to

him that there was something false about it,
a something unreal, as if she might have
locked his Madge up on bread and water
after a beating, and then scattered broadcast
the smooth information that "dear Madge is
coming presentlay."

It was really a great injustice to the little
widow, who, although she was not sorry that
Madge had but little inclination for the society
into which she had to take two girls with a
view to a suitable establishment for each, was
on the whole very good to her niece. She
would have, and had, utterly scouted the idea
that it was possible Madge could have any
attraction for the Honourable Marcus Orford ;
still she was quite as anxious to establish her
niece comfortably and suitably as she was in the
case of her daughters, only, as was but natural
with a mother, when such an unusually good establishment as that of the future Lord Cecspring
came within the range of possibility, she could
hardly be blamed for giving her daughters the
first place. But, of course, Marcus Orford,
judging her from his own standpoint, had not
the least idea of this.

He waited patiently for the " presentlay "
which would bring his Madge (or somebody
else's) back to the scene of sale and barter, but
he could not wait long enough. As a matter of
fact, Laura and she had gone home, so that they
might have a substantial meat tea together to

fit them for the crush and fatigue of the evening, when admittance would be only a shilling;
Julia taking their place at their stall until their
return, when she would go home and fortify
herself in the same manner with her mother,
and come back an hour later for the first evening concert.

Now it happened that Marcus Orford had,
in an evil moment, accepted an invitation to
dine with "ME" and his good lady at their
palace, and as he had to go back to barracks,
which lie on the opposite side of the town to
the episcopal residence, to dress himself in
garments suitable to the occasion, he had not
time to wait and see how long a period of time
the word "presently" meant in Mrs Traff's
vocabulary.

He did not particularly enjoy his evening,
though the Bishop's wife was as kind as possible to him, and the handshake of "ME," both
in greeting and speeding, conveyed the highest
appreciation and the warmest of friendly feelings. Still he was not happy; the daughter of
the house, who fell to his share for dinner, Miss
Victoria, was not Madge; and even if there had
been no such being as Madge, Miss Victoria
would not have taken his fancy, the kindness
and the handshake notwithstanding.

Then the following day he was on a tiresome
and tedious court-martial, which kept him a
fast and most unwilling prisoner till near dinner-

time, when, having a couple of men dining with him, he had to dress in good time to receive them. And the day following that he looked in at the bazaar again, but saw nothing of Madge, when he at once went off to the Winter Garden in the hope of finding her in her old place under the mulberry tree; but she was not there, and he blamed Mrs Traff' as the cause of it.

"Downy old cat!" he muttered savagely; "she's seen what I really want, and thinks if she keeps Madge out of my way she may palm that Laura off on to me;" which, between you and me, was simply absurd on the very face of it.

The day following that he, with five of his brother-officers, went off to a dance fifteen miles away in the country. All things considered, he enjoyed himself very well, but on the Saturday which came next, he was once more disappointed by trying the bazaar again, just at the hour when Madge and Laura had gone home for their substantial tea.

Sunday he had the usual church parade, and attended "the Parish" in the afternoon, after which he went into Mrs Traff's for the now customary cup of tea, but found such a crowd assembled there — the outcome of the bazaar week—and Madge so busy among the teacups, that he had not an opportunity of saying a single word to her, excepting on the uninteresting topics of sugar and cream.

Q

But happily on Monday morning he received the blessed and thrice-welcome news that he was granted leave of absence from the 16th to the 26th of the month.

"And now," said Marcus Orford, with a triumphant gesture, " now we'll see if we can't manage to circumvent Madam Traff'."

SIDELIGHT.

MISS MAULEVERER.

THE Misses Mauleverer were, as everyone knew, daughters of Mordecai in
Mrs Traff's eyes; but on one never-
to-be-forgotten occasion she had the extreme
felicity of being at hand when Lord Charterhouse innocently " put his foot into it " with the
eldest of the four spinsters, who still rigorously
kept up the fiction of being quite young things,
who needed the protection of a chaperon from
the wiles of that monster—*man*, though it is
quite certain that all the four had done their
very best to enrol themselves among the ranks of
the British matrons.

She chanced to be standing close to one of
them at a ball given by the officers of the Black
Horse, when Lord Charterhouse came up to
speak to her, and seeing Miss Mauleverer at
his hand turned and spoke to her also. Now
it happened that he had only seen her once

and confused her in his mind with a married lady whom he had taken in to dinner some weeks before; therefore it was not a very surprising thing, though the effect of it was so astounding that Mr Winks' heart fairly stood still within him, that he addressed her thus :—

"Oh, how d'you do? Full room, is it not? *And are your daughters here to-night?*"

For a moment there was a silence as dead as could be in the middle of a crowded ballroom; then the—young—lady turned to her partner, after casting a freezing look at Mr Winks.

"Will you take me back to my CHAPERON?" she said, in an awfully—I use the word advisedly—distinct voice; and so the unhappy Mr Winks was left stranded.

CHAPTER XX.

BEHIND THE SCENES.

THE 17th had come, and rose upon the world a fair, bright, pleasant morn, just the day for pic-nic, water-party, or for the regimental sports of the 25th, better known as " The Black Horse."

Overhead there shone a good, honest, open-faced sun; a gentle breeze blew softly from the south. On the face of many a bold dragoon was the sunshine of coming success, in the heart of many a fair damsel was a gentle fluttering at the prospect of—well, a very pleasant afternoon.

But on one countenance in the old city of Blankhampton there was a cloud, a very black one! A certain little perky nose looked perkier than ever, a certain little sharp chin—by reason of the lips above it being more tightly shut than usual — looked sharper and more determined

even than its wont, and a certain high-pitched
voice, with a squeak in it, was more rasping
and discordant than any officer in the whole of
the garrison had ever had the—the—*the privilege*
of hearing it.   To be sure, the privilege was not
extended to any of the garrison at that moment,
for Mrs Traff' was safe in the bosom of her own
family.   Poor Mrs Traff', it was too bad that
she had refused two invitations to the sports
because she had accepted Orford's.   She didn't
know, how should she? that both of them had
been given *after* his—and here was a letter of
excuse, beginning, " My dear Mrs Trafford, I am
very sorry—and I hope you will not be very
angry with me—but most important and urgent
business takes me away for a few days, so that
I must ask you, as a very great favour, to forgive me for not being able to receive you in
person at our sports to-morrow."

" I nev-ah knew *any* thing so utterly annaw
ing in all my life," burst out Mrs Traff, laying
down the letter and looking with vexed eyes
—very wide open—at Julia.

" Awfully vexing," said Julia.   " But I daresay
some of the others will ask us.   What else does
he say ? "

" But I hope," her mother continued, reading
from the letter, " that my absence will not keep
you away, as my quarters will be all ready to
receive you, and Sir Anthony Staunton will be
there to entertain you for me.   If it is a fine

day, I feel sure you will enjoy the sports. Believe me, my dear Mrs Trafford, yours very sincerely. MARCUS ORFORD."

"Oh, Sir Anthony Staunton!" commented the little widow, in a mollified tone. "Well, of course, that makes it very different."

"I would sooner have Sir Anthony of the two!" exclaimed Laura. "He's such fun."

"Mr Gabrielli will be there," said her sister as a reminder.

"Ye-es! But—" brightening up somewhat —"but not in Captain Orford's rooms."

"No. I daresay not. But, Laurie, are you tired of him already? What a fickle person you are."

"No, I don't think I am"—not altogether denying the soft impeachment — "but Sir Anthony is great fun, and that Mr Gabrielli is rather heavy on hand. He wants such a lot of drawing out."

As a matter of fact, Mr Evelyn Gabrielli had shown in such a very unmistakable fashion that he did not want to marry Mrs Traft's youngest flower, that Miss Laura began to feel any little attentions given to him were but so much wasted ammunition, so much powder and shot expended, which had utterly failed to send the bullet anywhere near the bull's-eye. Just at first she had thought him handsome and rather nice, but during the last few days she had altered her mind completely, and now thought

him neither one nor the other. To be Lady
Staunton now would suit her exactly, and so
she repeated with a good deal of zest that Sir
Anthony was great fun.

"He's frightfully poor," said Julia, who, like
her mother, had a keen eye to the main chance.

"Ow, yes, my de-ah!" put in Mrs Traff, in her
most florid accents, "but has *great* expectations.
*Cap*tain Orford told me so only the oth-ah day!
Sir *A*nthony has two rich *old* aunts—*enor-*
mously wealth-ay"—in her desire to express
the extent of the wealth in question, Mrs Traff's
accent acquired a richness of tone and colour
which far, far outshone the mellifluous tones of
Mrs Hugh Antrobus.

"Oh, I didn't know that, mother," from Julia.

"That makes him all the nicer," cried Laura,
who in her mind's eye began to see herself Lady
Staunton, and gave willing room for a thought
which flashed into her mind at that moment,
that perhaps Captain Orford had not *wanted* to
go away at all, but had only gone to oblige his
friend, and give him an opportunity of spending
all the afternoon in her company. It was absurd, of course, yet it made Miss Laura tread
upon air, and take her way barrackwards with
a heart bent upon enjoying the afternoon's entertainment to the uttermost.

"I wonder who is asking Lady Mainwaring,"
said Mrs Traff, helping herself to strawberry
jam, and, since the little annoyance about the

afternoon had been so successfully dispersed, speaking in quite her ordinary breakfast-time voice.

"Mr Brookes," answered Laura.

"Mr Brookes," in an accent of surprise. "Oh! really! Dear me, he seems to be quite Lady Mainwaring's—"

"Tame cat," finished Laura flippantly. "Oh! not a bit of it; don't you believe it for a moment. Margaret Damerel told me all about it yesterday."

"Yes, and what was that?"

"I'll tell you *all* about it," said Laura.

Now it happened that Margaret Damerel had struck up a violent friendship with Mrs Traff's youngest flower, and it happened also that her sister—"*that* Elizabeth," as poor Lester Brookes in the vexation of his heart had called her a few days previously—was afflicted with a temper which at times was the very reverse of amiable, so that now and again the two girls had a regular flare-up, in which Margaret, being the weaker of the two, invariably got the worst of it. On such occasions she, when Elizabeth went into sulks, sought out a confidant into whose ears she poured all her wrongs and a full and detailed list of all Elizabeth's shortcomings.

And as it happened, only a few days previously—to be accurate, on the very day of the reception at the Mansion House, Elizabeth, maddened by discovering the uselessness

of keeping a nice, comfortable velvet-covered
seat for a man who wouldn't sit down upon it
because she was there, had picked a quarrel
with the long-suffering Margaret, and the sisters
had not spoken since, which, " between you and
I," as Mrs Hugh said when she heard of it,
" must have been particularly pleasant and cosy
for dear Lady Mainwaring, who was doing *her*
best for both her nieces."

"Not having spoken since," meant that the
charming Elizabeth had not spoken *civilly;* for
when she was offended with Margaret, she was
not accustomed to keep silence—rather the contrary. But her speech consisted of continual
bickering, fault-finding, taunting, and gibing,
and sneering ; and, indeed, Lester Brookes was
not far wrong in the instinct which made him
speak of her as " *that* Elizabeth Damerel."

And this time, as she had managed to put
Lady Mainwaring out of conceit with Margaret,
the poor girl had poured her indignant con-
fidences into Laura Trafford's sympathetic ear.
So it was that Miss Laura was able to enlighten
her mother as to the position occupied by Lester
Brookes in the house of Lady Mainwaring.

" *I* believe he likes Margaret best," asserted
Laura. " Anyway, he hates Elizabeth."

" But how came he to ask them to his quarters
for the sports ? " Miss Traff' asked.

" Oh ! he didn't ; Margaret told me all about
it. Lady Mainwaring asked the Colonel to ask

them, but the Colonel couldn't, or wouldn't; said he had given his rooms to Sir Andrew's people; and then Lady Mainwaring made such a fuss, that Colonel Urquhart coolly offered her Mr Brookes's rooms, which are just over his."

"I would be ashamed to go to places, if I had taken such means to be asked to them," cried Lady Mainwaring's friend in high disdain.

"Oh! Lady Mainwaring's a very cool person," Julia declared. "Quite what you might expect from her class."

"Oh, yes! Because she's got a sort of a title," exclaimed Mrs Traff', closing her eyes in her most well-bred manner—"after all, only a *given* title, a sop to Sir Albert for putting the bridge over the channel—she really seems to think *any*thing becomes her. It is the greatest mistake—and really I don't think things should be made so equal! When engineers and prominent doctors, and ex-mayors and sheriffs, and so on, must be publicly recognised, I don't really think it is necessary they should have the same titles as the nobility. For instance, Lady Mainwaring is addressed just the same as if she were a Marchioness or Countess, which is too absurd. There certainly ought to be a difference. Instead of making baronets of such people, they might be made Justice! I think that would be a very good plan, and then everybody would understand that the title was only a public recognition of professional services, and there would be no need for the wives to give themselves airs about it. It would sound well—

"Justice and Madam Mainwaring!"

"But why 'Justice'?" said Laura.

"Because I don't think of anything better at this moment," returned Mrs Traff', sharply. "They might be called 'Worthy'—that would have a nice *respectable* sound about it, which would quite prevent their ever getting mixed up with the aristocracy."

"They might call them Master and Madam," suggested Laura with a laugh.

"Yes; the Most Worthy Master and Madam," cried Mrs Traff', eagerly. "I'm sure it would become Lady Mainwaring a great deal better than her present dignity, which she always carries as if she had been born in the purple. For my part, I have no sympathy for assumption in any shape or form. What was it that Mr du Maurier's clever creation Mrs Ponsonby de Tompkins said? 'They say we are always the hardest on the faults we have most strongly ourselves?' Oh! that is not true; for if I have a horror of *any*thing, it is of *worldliness*."

Those may not be the very words, but they convey Mrs Traff's meaning (and mine) to a nicety.

SIDELIGHT.

MISS GRANTLEY.

IN Blankhampton she was most often called "the young lady with the nose." She was *not* a nice girl, and she had shockingly bad manners. Her temper was atrocious, and she was very delicate; so delicate, that her nerves, her lungs, her eyes her head, her whole neighbourhood, her everything had to be considered first, before anybody else.

Besides being delicate, she posed as being very good, and if heading her letters with all the saints' days or their eves, and other such practices, shows great goodness, why, she was good—exceedingly.

But once Marcus Orford came to be a little enlightened on the subject, and it was in this wise. He was going to make a call upon her mother, but just as he reached the pretty rustic

porch of their house, a voice came from within
—the voice of Mrs Grantley.

"Really, Mabel, I am surprised at you, quarrel-
ing with Jack again! Why cannot you let the
boy alone? I do not know," with a great sigh,
"where your unfortunate temper will end in
leaving you."

"I don't get my temper from my *father*,"
retorted the young lady with the nose, with a
crushing accent of conviction, which sent Marcus Orford into a fit very nearly, ere he could
muster up sufficient calmness to pull the bell a
second time.

And presently the young lady with the nose
came to him in the pretty shaded drawing-room,
and asked him, "as darling mother is lying
down with a headache, to excuse her!"

CHAPTER XXI.

SUNSHINE AFTER RAIN.

UP at the Cavalry Barracks all was bustle and busy movement. Men were hard at work marking out courses, polishing arms and accoutrements, grooming such horses as would be wanted for the full-dress competition, in which a number of troopers would test how soon a man could be from jersey and drawers, garbed in all the glory of full-dress and be seated in the saddle.

Officers were touching up their rooms and decking them with flowers and plants, so as to show them to the best advantage in the eyes of the fair visitors who were coming to see the sports. And such vendors of eatables as had leave to trade within the barracks, had brought their carts—and their donkeys too, for there was a chance of turning an honest penny in hiring them out for the donkey-race—and were spreading out their wares in the most tempting way, piles of apples and nuts, plums and pears, and great heaps of more or less sticky lollipops, backed by the gay and lively ginger beer, and the light and frolicsome lemonade.

In the officers' quarters were various sensations and moving motives among the men passing to and fro in the different rooms. There was Colonel Urquhart in his sitting-room, standing with his back to the fireplace, while his servant and the provost-sergeant's wife, who had given an eye to the keeping of his quarters ever since he had been in the regiment, made a perfect bower for the reception of the General's wife and her party.

" Just a few more flowers in there, sir," she entreated.

" All right—it will look like a Jack in the green, or a butcher's shop at Christmas," returned Urquhart.

" Oh, no, sir ; I'm sure the ladies will say it looks lovely ! " Mrs Dean exclaimed.

" Perhaps they will. I'll tell you if they do," the Colonel answered.

Overhead " Young Pitch-and-Toss," as they called him in the regiment, was saying to his servant in disgusted accents, " Just shove those pictures out of sight, Jackson, and take all those books into Mr Crompton's quarters ; and —er—oh ! d— that old woman ! "—in an aside to himself—" and—er—I suppose you better go down to Mrs Forrest's and get some flowers to stick about. And, by-the-bye, can't you get Mrs Green to sew up the rag iu that curtain? Yes. Well, you'd better do it then, and just shove my boots and things out of sight, and make the place look as decent as you can." And then, when Jackson had growled out a "Yessir," he "d—d that old woman" again, just by way of giving vent to his outraged and disgusted feelings, and went out of his quarters leaving Jackson in delighted and intense amusement.

"Seems to me," he growled to his comrade Strong, Mr Crompton's servaut, when he went iuto that gentleman's quarters at the back of the house with an armful of books for which he wanted shelter, including three large photograph albums and two scrap-books, which Brookes did not choose to leave under the fair Elizabeth's sharp eyes,—"seems to me as 'ow my master don't care so very much about 'is company this arternoon. 'E didn't mean me for to catch it, but all the same I 'eard him say, 'Damn that ole woman,' more than once. It's plain 'e don't want 'er to be poking 'er nose inside of these 'ere halbums."

"I dessay not," responded Strong. "If my master's quarters had been at the front, I should 'ave gort myself put iu 'orspital for something or other; for you've no end o' trouble, and never a tip from all the 'ole blooming lot."

R

In the larger block of officers' quarters exchange had also taken place. Sir Anthony Staunton had just strolled into Orford's quarters to see if all was right—as Orford had put it, "Just look in before they come, old fellow, and see the place is pretty fit," so there he was doing this friendly duty. In his quarters beneath, young Charterhouse was in possession, as busy as the proverbial bee, and the result was so charming that had Staunton's aunt, Miss Lavinia, been there to see, it is not impossible, no, nor even in the least improbable, that not all Urquhart's ingenuity and all Archie Falconer's bright wit could have prevented her from then and there taking up her residence in Blankhampton Barracks for an unlimited period, even extending to practically a permanence.

"Why, Mr Winks," cried the owner of the rooms when he came back from his inspection of Orford's quarters, "what a palace you've made of the place! Bless my soul! I never thought to see my rooms looking anything like this."

"Oh! I don't know; I've only brought one or two little ornaments of my own to lighten the place up a bit; your quarters are rather bare, you know," returned Mr Winks, looking round all the time with an air of honest pride.

"Bare! ye gods, yes, that's true. I started with a stock of pretty-pretties, but they all came to grief long ago, got smashed up by the first few moves I made. What's this? Wall mirror, with yellow laburnums and lilac upon it Whatever made you buy such a gimcrack thing as that?"

"Oh! a girl painted that for me," answered Mr Winks carelessly.

"Oh! a girl—eh? And where did you get this?" pointing to a smart satin and lace wall pocket made on a palm leaf.

"Oh! another girl made me that," returned Mr Winks. "Awfully useful thing. Look here, I put a drop of water in this little flat pot, and then any amount of flowers stick into it. Good idea, isn't it?"

"Very good! By Jove! that's a handsome girl."

"Yes—ain't she? She's my cousin."

"Oh! Married?"

"Married! No, of course not. Does she *look* as if she was married?"

"Well, no, perhaps not; but that's neither here nor there. Did *she* carve the frame?"

"Yes, I believe she did,"—unwillingly.

"Oh, she did. Ah! by-the-bye, who are you entertaining to-day?"

"Mr and Miss Antrobus."

"Nobody else?"

"Yes, some visitors of theirs."

"Ah! By-the-bye, are you going to marry Miss Antrobus?"

Mr Winks looked up sharply—very sharply.

" Eh ? " said he in a questioning tone.

" Are you going to marry her ? " Staunton repeated.

" I don't know," said Mr Winks, after a moment's pause ; and then a moment later added, " It's not at all improbable."

Staunton stared straight at him for a moment without speaking. Then, as it were, he shook himself free of some recollections, and broke the silence.

" Oh, well, of course, Winks, it's no business of mine whether you mean to marry Miss Antrobus or not. Only, I've heard a good deal about her in my time, so perhaps it was that made me speak without thinking." And then, without giving Mr Winks time to reply, Staunton turned sharply round and fairly bolted out of the room.

But Mr Winks stood still, staring at his cousin's photograph for full ten minutes.

" Now, what the devil did he mean by that ? " he said aloud at last. " ' Heard a good deal about her in his time.' Yes ; but the question is *what* has he heard ? "

However, the time for the arrival of the company was close at hand, so that Lord Charterhouse has no choice but to slip into his plain clothes, and make all haste so as to be ready to receive his visitors ; and even as he gained the neatly-gravelled space in front of the officer's quarters, the carriage containing the first of the guests of the day turned in at the gates, and came rapidly towards them.

In this sat the General's wife, wearing a resplendent gown and coat of crimson plush, which looked a trifle warm for the day, but was a great compliment to the sports. Beside her sat a lovely girl, whom half-a-dozen fellows went forward to greet, though none remained to chat as long as the beautiful face deserved; this was the Dean's daughter, Miss Adair.

On the opposite seat was the General, a man of fine presence, some thirty years older than the good lady in the crimson gown. There was a general rush of officers to speak to him. "Good morning, General!" "Good day, General!" "How are you, sir?" and so on, while in each heart there was a joyful chuckle to think that they had got the better of him in the matter of uniform. For the previous month an order had gone round that no officer was to be seen outside of barracks except in uniform, and these were the sports *in* barracks and the officers of the Black Horse were to a man in mufti! Consequently the General was, as a cheeky young subaltern put it in a whisper to Mr Winks, "completely done in the eye."

The next to arrive on the scene was Lady Mainwaring, with the Damerol girls in her train. So poor Lester Brookes had to go on the rack at once, though he avenged himself on "*that* Elizabeth" by attaching himself persistently to Margaret, not a little to that young lady's delight, though she knew—no one better—that she would have to suffer for it afterwards; still, under the circumstances,—for the sisters had not made friends yet, and Elizabeth's temper that morning had been more unfortunate than usual—her triumph was not to be wondered at nor greatly condemned. And she *did* take it out of Elizabeth—no mistake about it.

And then came Mrs Trafford, with her two flowers, and after her a host of other people, who have nothing to do with this story, including the young lady with the nose under convoy of Mrs Mornington-Brown.

Mrs Traff' was light and sweetness itself to her proxy host. She at once set about making Blankhampton pleasant to him as she had done for Marcus Oxford; but somehow she did not seem to get on with him quite so well as she could have wished. He was very polite and attentive and everything of that sort, and yet she felt as if she was at arm's length and would never be able to approach nearer. She felt at last half afraid of him, and began to wish he would go away, and let some of the others—with spirits more congenial than his to a lonely little widow woman, who wanted everybody to be happy — come and entertain them. But no, Sir Anthony had promised Marcus Orford to entertain the little widow in his stead, there-

fore to the little widow he stuck like grim
death or a bad husband, and never a ghost of
a chance had any one else! But she was a
brave little woman, and never showed a sign of
her disappointment.

"Oh, there's Colonel Urquhart!" she exclaimed, as the commanding officer crossed the
broad pathway beneath the windows of Orford's
sitting-room. "*What* is he going to do, I
wonder? What a beautiful dog that is of his!
Dear old fellow! How I should have liked to
bring my colley with me, but I thought he would
get in the road and perhaps be a trouble."

"Oh, yes, dogs are a great nuisance at affairs
of this kind," said Sir Anthony, forgetting that
Mrs Traff' had special reasons for treasuring the
dear colley. "Yes, they get in the road of
every one, and get kicked and trodden on,
and made miserable all round. Oh, they're far
better at home—far better. I shut both my
dogs up before anybody came."

"Oh, you have dogs?"

"Yes—a bull-terrier and a mastiff. But the
bull-terrier is a terrible beggar to fight, and
the other hates a crowd of any kind ; so I shut
them both up out of harm's way."

"Oh, yes, it was much better. It is dreadful when they fight," Mrs Traff' cried. "And
your mastiff does not like a crowd?"

"Hates it. Now the Colonel's dog, Zug, is a
very amicable fellow, who can take care of him-

self under all or any circumstances. Some dogs are like that. Is yours?"

"Oh, no, not all—he is quite a baby—not quite ten months old. Colonel *Ur*quhart gave him to me."

"Oh, really!" and then Staunton recalled to mind all he had heard concerning that same colley pup, and wished he had not asked the question.

"Is Colonel Urquhart entertaining to-day?" Mrs Traff' asked suddenly.

"Yes—Lady Hamilton, and some friends of hers. By-the-bye, Miss Adair came with her."

"Oh, yes, she said yesterday, you know dears, that Lady Hamilton was going to bring her. Oh, I must go and speak to them before we leave. Why, there is Mrs An—trobus," in accents of profound surprise.

Sir Anthony glanced out to see the slender figure of his comrade, Charterhouse, walking between the fair Polly and her vast mother.

"Yes, they must have come out just to see something—perhaps the prizes. I lent Charterhouse my rooms; his quarters are at the back of this block."

Lord Charterhouse and his two guests went slowly across the green to the stand whereon were displayed the prizes of the day. Then, after lingering there a few minutes, they turned back and retraced their steps, disappearing beneath the arch of the principal

entrance into the building, but not before Mrs
Hugh had recognised Mrs Traff' sitting at the
window, and had greeted her with the friend-
liest of nods and wreathed smiles.

Poor little Mrs Traff'! After this *every*thing
seemed to go wrong. It was not often that
she felt herself neglected, yet she was wofully
left to herself that afternoon, literally to herself, for Sir Anthony Staunton paid all his attention to Miss Laura, sitting at one window
with her, while her mother and sisters shared
the other. Mrs Traff' did not so much mind
for herself—what mother really feels angry at
personal dulness if her daughters are having
plenty of enjoyment and admiration?—but she
felt that Julia was having but a very sorry
time. Nay, she more than felt; she saw by
the thunder-cloud upon that young lady's brow
that she deeply resented Laura's appropriation
of Sir Anthony Staunton. Of course it was all
very nice to have him wheel an exceedingly
cosy chair up to the window, and say, "Pray
try this chair, Miss Trafford, it's the most comfortable chair in Orford's rooms, except the one
your mother is sitting upon;" and it was very
nice to have him, after handing Orford's opera-
glass to Mrs Traff', go across the room and
bring another similar article of luxury off the
chimney-shelf, and say, "I lent Charterhouse
my rooms for this afternoon, but I didn't see
the fun of lending him my opera-glass, so I

brought it along." This was all very nice, but
then to have him betake himself to the other
window, where he and Laura could and did
lean their elbows on the sill in sweet and
pleasant familiarity, was altogether another
thing—altogether! Yes, Mrs Traff' was mother-
like, only too glad for Laura to be having a
good time, but she would have liked Julia to
be faring as well, and she certainly would
have been glad of somebody to chat with a
little herself; but I am afraid Miss Julia was
moved by no such sweet and unselfish motives;
like her mother, she would wish that Laura had
a good time, but *after her*. So the clouds upon
her not very fair brow grew thicker and thicker
—I use the word *thicker* advisedly—and the
expression of Mrs Traff's face grew more and
more anxious with each moment, for paraphras-
ing the song, "There's a good time coming
boys," she pretty well knew what to expect.

But small heed did the pair in the other window take of Julia's black looks or Mrs Traff's
anxious ones; for as Sir Anthony pointed out
which were men of his troop, which among
them were his favourites, which were black
sheep, and so on, the elbows somehow got
nearer and nearer to each other, until it was
impossible they could go any further. Then,
as time had considerably lessened space between them, it was not necessary to give his
information concerning the principal actors in

the drama below in such a loud voice as before. So, from hearing distinctly an interesting
little history, such as this,—"You see that
fellow over there—the one with the light
curly hair? Well, that fellow was at Oxford with me, awfully good sort he was too.
Yes, came a smasher and enlisted. His
name? Oh, well, I'd rather not tell you
his name, because no one else in the regiment
knows—they call him Charles Hammond now.
Not his real name? Oh, dear, no. You'd
know it in a minute if I could tell it to you,—
it's as well known a name in England as Glad-
stone's—" their conversation dwindled to a
" growl, growl, growl—chatter, chatter, growl,"
of which not one single word was distinguish-
able to mother and sister.

And then tea came up—" From the MESS,"
as Mrs Hugh would have put it in her
friendly call-every-goose-a-swan fashion, —
which rather smoothed matters over a little;
for Sir Anthony came over from his window
to do the honours, and Lester Brookes came
upstairs and joined them, true to his resolve,
that as the Colonel had chosen to invite people
to his quarters, he might entertain them
himself.

" How is it you're not having tea with your
ladies, Lester?" Sir Anthony inquired, hoping
to get him on to the subject of his grievances
in that respect.

"I haven't any ladies here. I didn't invite any one to the sports," he answered stolidly, handing a beautiful pile of hot-buttered muffins to Mrs Trafford.

"But Lady Mainwaring and her nieces are in your room."

"Oh, yes, of course; but they are the Colonel's guests—not mine. I only lent him my room because Lady Hamilton had asked for his."

"But have they any tea?"

"Oh yes. I sent tea up there, and then went and told the Colonel it was ready. It's all right, don't worry about them. Urquhart's up there now."

The three Trafford ladies heard this little conversation as they applied themselves to the buttered muffins; then three pairs of eyes exchanged glances of the most exquisite enjoyment, and still more of the crumpled rose leaves which had hitherto marred the pleasure of the afternoon were smoothed out, so that they began —all of them, that is—to find the regimental sports a very delightful kind of entertainment. And then three young gentlemen of the Blankshire Regiment found their way into the room, and Sir Anthony sent for a fresh relay of tea and muffins, and presently went back to his window, in company with Miss Laura, without so much as a wry look being cast after either of them.

There were still four or five items of the programme to be got through, so after consulting with Laura as to whether they were going out that evening, and finding that they were not doing so, Sir Anthony had a brief consultation with Orford's servant, with the result of a large basket of choice fruit and some champagne making their appearance, which had a marvellous effect in finishing off the smoothing process, and acted upon Julia's sharp little countenance very much as a hot flat-iron and a piece of flannel do upon a touch of lumbago in the small of your back.

"How do you go home, Mrs Trafford?" asked Sir Anthony, when it was all over, and they had watched Mrs Hugh and Polly drive away in an open cab, after taking the tenderest farewell of Lord Charterhouse.

"Oh! we will walk, I think; we don't dine till eight," Mrs Traff' answered, wondering what Laura's nods from behind meant.

"I'll walk down with you, if you will allow me?"

"Oh! we shall be delighted."

The other men also volunteered to walk as far as the town with them, so Mrs Traff' and her girls returned homewards in quite a triumphant procession; so much so, that Mrs Hugh and Polly, who had gone down to the High Street before turning into the River House, chancing to see them, said to one another—at least, Mrs Hugh said it to Polly, who agreed with her—that perhaps after all they hadn't gained anything at all by having a cab instead of using their legs like other folk.

"What is it, my dear?" Mrs Traff' asked at the first opportunity, keeping Laura's nods still in mind.

"Ask him to dinner."

"No."

"Yes; he wants to come. I'll tell you after. Ask him," was the hurried reply.

So Mrs Traff', when they reached her own door, and were watching Lester Brookes and the three young gentlemen of the Blankshire Regiment go gaily away towards the club, said airily to Sir Anthony,—

"I suppose it is no use asking you to come in and dine with us, just as we are?"

"Oh yes, indeed, Mrs Trafford, it is," he answered, eagerly.

That of course settled the question, and Mrs Traff' led the way into the house and upstairs into the drawing-room, where she drew back with a great start as soon as she put her nose within the door thereof.

"*Madge!*" she cried.

"*Madge!*" cried the girls, in a breath.

Then Mrs Traff's voice was heard again, crying in accents of profound astonishment,—

"CAPTAIN—ORFORD!"

SIDELIGHT.

CAPTAIN MURPHY.

IF Captain Murphy—otherwise Tempest, author of *The Gate of Paradise*, otherwise "The Wind"—had any pride, it was in his "style," as an author, that is. He was accustomed to give orations to anybody who would listen to him, on the subject of style. He could, and would, and did enlarge upon the respective merits of Charles Reade and Wilkie Collins, his two masters and models.

"Look at Wilkie Collins's stuff," he would say, "no pad, no iteration, no weakness; all strong, crisp, sparkling; not a word too much; never a long sentence where a short one will express his meaning; never a long word where he can use a short one; and the result—a master! See Charles Reade, look at *The Cloister and the Hearth, what* a book! See the style! You are not reading a modern novel; you are *living* walking, breathing the air and manners of the middle ages! And what does it, sir? Style, I tell you, style, and *style* alone."

"Which may be very true," confided Marcus Orford one day to Lester Brookes; "but I don't understand that sort of thing myself, and I'm rather tired of hearing about 'style.' I'm going to put a stop to it."

Therefore, about ten days later, and for some weeks afterwards, Murphy had the felicity of receiving, through an agent, a number of cuttings taken from newspapers of different parts of the country, as follows :—

"Our readers will be surprised to learn that the author of *The Gate of Paradise*, who writes under the name of Tempest, is not a cavalry officer, but a lady."

Imagine the delight of the wretched author, who plumed and prided himself on the sharp, crisp, pithy vigour of his " style !"

CHAPTER XXII.

AFTER ALL!

"YES, it is I, Aunt Marion," said Madge, in a very shy voice, and with a very shy look.

"Yes, Mrs Trafford, it is ME," supplemented Orford, in a glad and proud tone, and with an emphasis on the pronoun-personal worthy of the ponderous spiritual lord up at the Palace, and with a fine disregard of grammar equal to that of the little boys in the Ingoldsby Legends.

"My dear—what *does* it mean?" cried Mrs Traff", turning to stare blankly first at one and then at the other of them.

"Oh! Aunt Marion—I—" began Madge, coming a step forward, then a something rose suddenly in her throat and choked her, so that she stood before the little widow blushing a rich, lovely rosy-red, and hung her head

S

with a shy, half-shamed air, which told her secret to Staunton in a minute.

"It means, Mrs Trafford," said Marcus Orford, taking his sweetheart's hand, and standing very brave and upright to explain matters, and make his peace, "it means that I went away from Blankhampton yesterday feeling like Ishmael —a jealous fool—as if my hand was against every man, and every man's hand against mine; and I have come back to-day to ask you to forgive me for having, for a few days, numbered even you among my enemies, and also to give me Madge, and make me happy for ever."

"To give you *Madge?*" cried Mrs Traff', in accents of unlimited and profound surprise.

"If you please," said Orford modestly; "that is, if you haven't any particular objection."

For a moment Mrs Traff's brain utterly refused to think—to act—to work; it stood stock still like a watch that has run down, or as the sun in the heavens at the bidding of Joshua. Then, all in the flash of another moment, her mind went back to certain stinging, scathing remarks she had made to Madge about this very man. And now Madge would be able to laugh, sneer, jeer and gibe at her for all the rest of her life, if she should so choose: after all, it had been Madge who was the attraction to him in No. 7 St Eve's; and Madge, whom they had all thought beneath his notice, because she could not or would not see the

value or utility of getting to the very top of
the social tree in Blankhampton, was going to
be Marcus Orford's wife, and in time Lady
Ceespring, after all.

What a world it was! In all her life, Mrs
Traff' had never considered her niece a handsome girl until that moment—positively it came
upon her almost with as great a surprise as
finding the two together had done, that really
Madge was as lovely a girl as might easily
be found in a day's march. And then, all at
once, she realised too that Madge stood all
alone in a hard and weary world, and that
she had just come to a turning-point, when
she wanted to be petted and made much of—
so she went a step forward and stood on the
tips of her toes to perform this kind and
motherly office. If Madge had been of a carp-
ing turn of mind, she might at that moment
have remembered how many and many a time
she had felt a very real need of just such a
comforting and comfortable way of making her
look back with a shade less regret to the happy
half-Bohemian life she had left behind her when
she turned away from her father's grave. She
might have remembered, as clearly as Mrs
Traff' was doing that same instant, all that
had been said concerning the very man who
was holding her hand fast within his own—
she might have remembered that, now she had
somebody who would pet and make much of

her for ever, somebody who would love her
and stand between her and the whole world
firm and true, always, she did not really need
that there should be any change in her aunt's
manner towards her. Yes, it is true, she might
have remembered all these things, and a good
many others equally unpleasant. But she did
not. No; there are few injustices, injuries,
quarrels or misunderstandings, which a grave
will not heal; still there are some. But a
marriage—with the only son of a nobleman—
none! Mrs Traff's arms were open wide to
receive her, and should she,—who had hungered
for love, craved for it, yearned for it, from any
body or anything, from Mrs Traff' herself down
to that wretched colley-pup, which had got her
into trouble by nibbling her gowns into holes
and gnawing her gloves into tatters,—should
she reject it now that it had come at last, just
because she was never likely to want for love
again? No—a thousand times, no—so she laid
her happy head upon the little widow's shoulder
and just cried a little, a few delicious tears,
while Marcus Orford, as proud as Lucifer, and
as happy as a king, stood by and saw with
approving eyes; it is true that for a second
or so he felt just a shade queer—but that phase
of feeling only lasted for a moment, and was
gone almost before he knew that it had been
born.

And after this there was a general rejoicing

and congratulating. Mrs Traff' resigned Madge to the girls, and set to work on Orford, whom she called her dear boy, and kissed with such a lavish show of motherly affection, that he called himself the greatest of brutes that he had ever doubted her for a moment or had the smallest fear of her not doing the right thing by his darling. And then Staunton made himself a little more prominent, and shook his comrade's hand till both their arms ached.

"You'll ask me to be best man, old fellow?" said he heartily.

"Oh! to be sure—whom else should I ask?" was Orford's reply.

"Well, you might have wanted to ask Urquhart, you know."

"Not a bit of it. You knew first, so you shall have the pleasure of standing by me at the last. By-the-bye, Mrs Trafford, I hope this man did my duty properly for me to-day?"

"Oh! *de-ah*, yes. We *all* enjoyed the afternoon thoroughly," Mrs Traff' replied. "Did we not, de-ahs?"

"Oh! yes, Captain Orford," from Julia.

"It was quite lovely," from Laura, with a look at Sir Anthony, who returned it with interest—and then Mrs Traff' carried the three girls away, saying that dinner would be ready in five minutes.

What a merry meal it was! Just a little wee tiny bit scanty, as Mrs Traff' merrily explained. But what did that matter? What if they picked the bones of the plump dickey-bird clean, that Sir Anthony and Laura scarcely needed a finger-bowl after breaking the merry thought between them? Why, just nothing at all.

"Captain Orford," said little Mrs Traff' suddenly, during a pause in the laughter and fun, "why did you go away hating *me* of all people?"

Marcus Oxford turned a shade red under this straightforward question, and then he told her what he had overheard at the Mayoress's reception, and how far—at least *almost* how far—his jealous thoughts had led him.

"Oh! but I was only speaking of some pictures of her father's which I hold in trust, and which are to be sold after her marriage," she exclaimed.

"Ah! but I did not know that," he said, by way of extenuation.

"But why didn't you ask me at once?" she said wonderingly.

"Because I was a fool," said he promptly.

Mrs Traff' patted his hand indulgently.

"No—no—not a fool. Oh, no, but just a little wee bit foolish—eh?" she said sweetly.

Clever little Mrs Traff'!

"I think, dears," said, she a few hours later, "that when dear Madge is married, we will leave Blankhampton. Town will suit us better;

and, really, society here is very mixed. Lady
Mainwaring and her set are all very well, but
we should do just as well, if not better, without
them ; and, really, I think I can-*not* do with
that Mrs Antrobus. She's so very obtrusive
and familiar. I'm sure it would really be quite
a charity if someone would take that poor boy,
Lord Charterhouse, in hand, and get him away
from those people ; it would, indeed.

"I said something about it to — Marcus ;"
there was the very faintest hesitation before
she uttered the name, such as made Laura look
at Julia with exquisite enjoyment; "but he
said, 'Oh! trust Mr Winks to look after himself. His head's screwed on the right way—
no mistake about *that*.'"

"I am very glad to hear it," said Mrs Traff'
piously. "I am sure it is quite impossible to be
too careful in a garrison town, for society is so
very mixed, and it seems such a pity to think of
the Charterhouse title being wasted over such
a girl as that."

"Oh! I think she would look lovely in a
coronet!" cried Madge.

"Yes, my love, so would a wax dummy out
of a hairdresser's shop-window," replied Mrs
Traff' with decision ; "but that is not everything that is necessary to make such a marriage
suitable or proper.'"

.   .   .   .

It happened at that very moment that Mr Winks, having just left the mess-rooms for his quarters, was standing looking straight at himself in the glass over the fireplace.

"Mr Winks," said he aloud, "you're a fool! What do you want to be fooling after a pretty-faced muffin for, when you've got a cousin who's the handsomest and smartest girl in England, and adores you?"

Then he left the hearth and strode to the window, the curtain of which he pulled aside that he might look out into the star-lit night. "By Jove!" he exclaimed, "what a cad I am, to go running after that girl when—but there, it can't be helped now, but I'll put a stop to it altogether. I'll send in my papers to-morrow, and go straight up to town, and ask Nell to marry me at once. She will—I know she's fond of me, God bless her—and the other one is utterly incapable of ever being fond of any-one, so there's no harm done, though that's no fault of mine."

And then he got into his cot, and slept the sleep of the just.

Poor Polly! Poor Polly!

THE END.

COLSTON AND COMPANY, PRINTERS, EDINBURGH.

WORKS BY JOHN STRANGE WINTER.

ON MARCH.

F. V. WHITE & Co., LONDON.

Small Crown 8vo, Paper Covers, 1s.; Cloth, 1s. 6d.

Short Extracts from Opinions of the Press.

" The author of 'Bootles' Baby' and several other clever narratives of episodes in a cavalry officer's career, has allowed himself rather more scope in 'On March' than he has hitherto done. This short story is characterised by Mr Winter's customary truth in detail, humour, and pathos."—*Academy, April* 17, 1886.

"The versatility of the author's powers was never more strikingly shown."—*Broad Arrow, March* 27, 1886.

"By publishing 'On March,' Mr J. S. Winter has added another little gem to his well-known store of regimental sketches. The story is written with humour, and a deal of feeling."—*Army and Navy Gazette, March* 13, 1886.

"Not wanting in spirit and drollery."—*Morning Post, March* 12, 1886.

" A fascinating story, the reading of which will not be wasted time. The humour of the earlier chapter is very delicate, and in the pictures of childhood and girl-life, there is that which draws one to the writer as to a personal friend : it is the sportfulness of a pure, genial, manly nature."—*Birmingham Daily Post, March* 10, 1886.

"Dramatic in the extreme."—*Literary World, April* 9, 1886.

" Certainly one of the happiest efforts that have emanated from Mr Winter's prolific pen."—*Galignani's Messenger (Paris), March* 22, 1886.

"There is a wealth of pathos in the book."—*Colburn's United Service Magazine, April* 1886.

" Here we have another simple story of the personal life of the British man of war, by the genial author of ' Bootles' Baby.' Of course there are children amongst the actors in this new fable, and very pleasant ones too. But all Mr Winter's characters are pleasant, young or old."—*Hereford Times, March* 13, 1886

"In many points excels his previous productions."—*Toronto Weekly Mail, January* 28, 1886.

"A bright and vivacious story, wholesome in tone and sentiment."—*Nonconformist and Independent, March* 4, 1886.

"Another of the clever and fascinating stories by the author of 'Bootles' Baby,' 'Houp-la!' and other works now familiar wherever the English language is read."—*Scottish Reformer, March* 6, 1886.

"The characters are depicted true to the life, and the narrative, which is highly amusing, is told in that easy and lively style which so pre-eminently characterises this author's writings."—*Bookseller, March* 5, 1886.

"Will probably be as popular as any of its predecessors."—*Society, March* 27, 1886.

"We cannot praise the pathos of the concluding chapters too much. . . . Altogether, we can safely say that 'On March' fully deserves all the popularity accorded to the author's former works."—*Englishman (India), March* 29, 1886.

"'By the author of "Bootles' Baby"' is quite enough recommendation for any tale."—*South Durham Mercury, March* 27, 1886.

"The book is one of good intent, points an excellent moral, and cannot be laid aside without leaving a definite impression behind."—*Yorkshire Post, March* 24, 1886.

"Mr J. S. Winter writes in a most racy way of military life. He seems to have a thorough knowledge of garrison men and manners."—*Dover Chronicle, April* 10, 1886.

"The author of 'Bootles' Baby' will always command respectful attention, and in his pathetic little story 'On March,' Mr J. S. Winter has struck a chord which will vibrate sadly enough in the hearts of many of the women who read the life history of Allan Hastings, the so-called 'Man of Honour.'"—*Lady's Pictorial, April* 1, 1886.

"Written in a lively and vivacious style."—*Aberdeen News, March* 27, 1886.

"The author of 'Bootles' Baby,' it may be said, owes much success to a certain happy facility of expression, and an unaffected skill in depicting military life, with the various phases of which much familiarity is shown. In 'On March,' these features are as prominent as ever."—*Publisher's Circular, March* 1, 1886.

CAVALRY LIFE.

Short Extracts from Opinions of the Press.

"'Cavalry Life' is one of the best books of its kind that we have seen. Full of 'go,' and the style is easy and lively."-- *Saturday Review, January 14, 1882.*

"The author possesess no mean literary power, and, what is just as essential to success in book-making, a happy, hearty spirit."—*St James's Gazette, January 23, 1882.*

" Here is a writer as intimately acquainted with the inner life and *camaraderie* of barracks as he is with the management of his charger and the evolutions of cavalry."—*The World, March 29, 1882.*

"'Cavalry Life' is a book which does one good to read, a manly, even in a certain sense a noble book."—*The Morning Post, April 12, 1882.*

"The writer has no doubt served, and has based his plots upon his experiences in military life."—*Monthly Military Budget, January, 1882.*

"Perhaps his volumes may not merely divert, but achieve a useful purpose in correcting the romantic and sentimental view of the cavalry officer, which finds favour among so many lady novelists in these days."—*The Daily News, April 10, 1882.*

"The whole tone and contents of the book are unimpeachably moral. Just the thing for a dull afternoon."—*Graphic, January 28, 1882.*

" The author seems to have been a cavalry officer, and to know intimately what he writes about. There is not one syllable to which the most scrupulous can take exception ; while there is a current of liveliness, brightness, and manliness of tone running throughout the whole."—*Scotsman, January 24, 1882.*

"Sketches and stories capitally told by a cavalry officer and well suited to please the taste of every class of reader."—*Army and Navy Gazette, January 28, 1882.*

" The author also has the power of depicting pathetic scenes with taste and truth, and with no introduction of false senti- ment."—*The Standard, April 7, 1882.*

" We unhesitatingly declare that it is one of the liveliest and most amusing works we have read for a long time past."—*Civil Service Gazette, February 4, 1882.*

"He is often vigorous, and he is never wearisome."—*Leeds Mercury, February 8, 1882.*

REGIMENTAL LEGENDS.

Short Extracts from Opinions of the Press.

"Light and lively; they sketch soldiers and their ways and manners from the life, and ought to be popular in mess ante-rooms, and officers' quarters . . . The style is invariably easy and gentlemanly."—*The Times, February* 8, 1883.

"When we say that the whole three volumes are entirely original and clever, we afford praise requiring not another word in addition."—*The Monthly Military Budget, February* 1883.

"They throw well into the foreground the kindly fellowship, the gay good humour, and the unfaltering courage of British officers."—*Daily News, December* 29, 1882.

"Mr Winter knows what he is writing about. He has had experience of the life which he described. There is not one story which will not deeply interest the reader. There will be a desire to hear from Mr Winter again. He has whetted the appetite of the public, and he will have to find more stories like these to meet the demand that he has raised."—*Scotsman, December* 26*th*, 1882.

"They are good, honest, soldier-like stories."—*The Standard, January* 18, 1883.

"As lively and dramatic as any that appeared in 'Cavalry Life.' "—*The Broad Arrow, December* 16, 1882.

"They are written in a free-and-easy style, with a certain dash and rollic about them, and are pleasant reading . . . The glimpses of soldiers' lives both in India and at home will, as professional life always does, interest many."—*British Quarterly Review, January* 1883.

"All of them are pleasant, lively, and readable. We hope it will not be long before Mr Winter brings out another similar delightful set."—*Glasgow Herald, February* 1, 1883.

"More amusing, accurate, and readable soldier stories we never remember to have read."—*York Herald, December* 27, 1882.

"The writer has already made good his footing in the literary world by his 'Cavalry Life' and in this publication has made prodigious advance."—*The Tablet, December* 23, 1882.

"Mr Winter depicts with striking vividness and many touches of real pathos."—*The Literary World, February* 16, 1883.

"A collection of amusing stories."—*United Service Gazette, January* 27, 1883.

BOOTLES' BABY.

Short Extracts from Opinions of the Press.

"Miss Mignon is a delightful little bit of childhood."—*Saturday Review, July* 25, 1885.

"A succession of capital sketches of military life and manners. The various characters depicted are true to the life."—*Broad Arrow, June* 27, 1885.

"This little story is perhaps the brightest, most pathetic, and interesting of the many that have emanated from the pen of the author."—*Admiralty and Horse Guards Gazette, June* 13, 1885.

"Mr Winter's pictures of military life are always excellent." —*British Quarterly Review, July* 1885.

"A capital story, full of 'go' and interest. It never allows the attention of the reader to flag, and it is thoroughly wholesome and amusing."—*Scotsman July* 3, 1885.

"Bright, lively, manly, spirited, and thoroughly enjoyable throughout."—*Birmingham Daily Post, September* 2, 1885.

"The book could hardly be better."—*Glasgow Herald, July* 1, 1885.

"'Bootles' Baby' is a model short story. . . . It can have few equals."—*Yorkshire Post, August* 26, 1885.

"'Bootles' Baby' is unapproachable."—*Bristol Mercury, August* 15, 1885.

"Written with the author's acknowledged raciness and humour."—*Civil Service Gazette, June* 13, 1885.

"The blending of true humour and genuine pathos in the tale makes it delightful reading."—*Manchester Courier, August* 14, 1885.

"His sketches of military life are inimitable, and 'Bootles' Baby' is one of the best." —*Publishers' Circular, June* 15, 1885.

"One of the most charming stories we have met with for some time."—*Northern Echo, June* 8, 1885.

"A charming little story of military life."—*New York Sun.*

"It is finely told, with humour and pathos, and excels in quick character drawing and style. It moves the better feelings."— *Boston Globe.*

HOUP-LA!

Short Extracts from Opinions of the Press.

"'Houp-la' is a good story."—*Saturday Review, August* 22, 1885.

"In this novelette we have a striking proof of the author's insight into the deeper side of human nature. . . . In 'Houp-la' the author has achieved a distinct success."—*Naval and Military Gazette, September* 7, 1885.

"Mr Winter writes very pleasantly and always with full knowledge of his subject. His officers are the officers of the present day."—*St James's Gazette, September* 1, 1885.

"It proves that he can not only write in an easy and lively style which carries his readers along with him, but that he has also at his command a fund of true pathos."—*The Morning Post, September* 11, 1885.

"One of the most beautiful little stories recently given to the world is 'Houp-la.'"—*Lady's Pictorial, August* 22, 1885.

"Will certainly keep up the reputation which 'Bootles' Baby' and earlier books have won for the author as a delightful describer of cavalry life and manners."—*Glasgow Herald, September* 4, 1885.

"A wholesome, well-written, capitally-told story with good incident."—*Scotsman, September* 16, 1885.

"His pathos and his humour are alike unforced."—*Manchester Courier, August* 21, 1885.

"The charm of Mr Winter's stories is in their simplicity, their genuine human sympathy, and their constant liveliness and humour."—*Hereford Times, August* 15, 1885.

"The tale is touchingly written, and the incidents and conversation show that the author is well up in military life."—*Newcastle Courant, August* 14, 1885.

"Some of the most delightful stories of military life to be found in modern fiction. 'Bootles' Baby' and 'Houp-la' are among the most deservedly popular of shilling volumes."—*The Whitehall Review, October* 1, 1885.

"A very strong little story which has much genuine pathos."—*Weekly Chronicle, San Francisco, November* 22, 1885.

"A simple, affecting tale of humble fidelity and affection."—*New York Times, October* 23, 1885.

"The author displays the skill of a real artist."—*Otago Times, N.Z., December* 26, 1885.

"A story of adventure, exciting situations, strange scenes, odd characters, and of absorbing interest."—*Albany Press, U.S.A.*

WORKS BY JOHN STRANGE WINTER.

IN QUARTERS.

F. V. WHITE & Co., LONDON.

(Small Crown 8vo, Paper Covers, 1s. ; Cloth, 1s. 6d.)

Short Extracts from Opinions of the Press.

" ' In Quarters' is one of those rattling tales of soldiers' life which the public have learned to thoroughly appreciate."—*The Graphic, December* 12, 1885.

" The author of 'Bootles' Baby' gives us here another story of military life, which few have better described."—*British Quarterly Review, January* 1886.

" Those who have read Mr J. Strange Winter's previous works will know that there is pleasure in store for them in the perusal of his new story ' In Quarters.' . . . His intimate knowledge of the inner life of barracks renders his tales of soldiers and their ways accurate, whilst they are, without exception, bright and amusing."— *The Morning Post, January* 6, 1886.

" In the best sense of the word, human, and may be warmly commended."—*Broad Arrow, March* 27, 1886.

" Will be received with pleasure by the entire English-speaking public. 'In Quarters' is simply a mighty shilling's worth of amusement."—*Sunday Times, December* 6, 1885.

" ' In Quarters' consists of a series of 'Chronicles of the 25th (The Black Horse) Dragoons,' written in the delightful style of 'Bootles' Baby' and other works by the author. Though it has not the charm of a continuous narrative, it is sure to receive a cordial welcome."—*The Literary World, November* 27, 1885.

" In every way decidedly one of the best things provided for Christmas reading."—*Public Opinion, November* 20, 1885.

" This pleasant volume of military tales will doubtless be as deservedly popular as its author's previous productions."—*Court Circular, January* 30, 1386.

" Short, stirring, and full of incident, they will please all, while offending none."—*The Weekly Times, December* 13, 1885.

" Like the author's former works, it deals with military incidents, and these are presented in a form that should render the book exceedingly popular."—*Publishers' Circular, December* 7, 1885.

" Written in the spirited, vivacious, sparkling style, which is characteristic of the author—a writer who has recently come to the front with a rush. . . . Very, very funny are some of the episodes ; thrilling, horrible, terrible in the extreme are others. Needless to say, the book is exceedingly interesting— bright, pleasing, natural."—*The Western Morning News, December* 28, 1885.

" The chronicles are really first-class stories, narrated with a natural force which is fascinating, and genuinely pathetic or humorous, as the circumstances chance to demand."—*Edinburgh Daily Review, December* 19, 1885.

" The style is easy and lively, and the author shows that full acquaintance with military life and manners which has distinguished his previous productions."—*The Bookseller, December* 15, 1885.

" As usual, Mr Winter shows a thorough knowledge of barrack life in a cavalry regiment."—*The Glasgow Herald, January* 9,1886.

" Many Christmas books have reached us, but this is the best of all. Here, indeed, we have true wit and humour and pathos, and all that is needed to make up a most delightful little volume."—*The Hants Telegraph, December* 12, 1885.

" It consists of ten chapters, in which are narrated amusing, funny, pathetic, and even tragic incidents. . . . The author aims, he says, at being light. Whether light or heavy, he is always readable."—*Newcastle Weekly Courant, November* 27, 1885.

" A chatty little volume abounding in the record of practical jokes."—*The Yorkshire Post, December* 2, 1885.

" The author has already become a popular writer on such subjects with ' Bootles' Baby,' ' Houp-la,' and other books. This one, ' In Quarters,' is at least equal to either of them in interest." —*Bath Journal, December* 26, 1885.

" There is not within the covers of the volume a single dull page."—*Richmond Chronicle, December* 5, 1885.

" Mr Winter's style is most attractive, and every story that he relates is most engagingly told."—*The Western Mercury, November* 26, 1885.

" ' In Quarters ' is one of those capital soldier stories in which J. S. Winter delights ; stories, too, which also delight his readers."—*Court and Society, December* 7, 1885.

" A military novel of exciting situations."—*Albany Sunday Press, N.Y., November* 22, 1885.

" The narrative is unflaggingly interesting, and at times very dramatic."—*Commercial Advertiser, N.Y., December* 1, 1885.

" A spirited sketch of military life."—*The Telegram, N.Y., December* 8, 1885.

" A collection of short stories, both jovial and pathetic. All are brief and slight, but briskly narrated in the dashing manner of the author."—*Boston Herald, U.S.A., December* 7, 1885.

" Mr Winter gives us some more of his graphic sketches of cavalry life in his recently published ' In Quarters,' a series of tales, all told in his usual excellent style."—*Auckland Chronicle, N.Z., December* 18, 1885.

" A captivating story of military life."—*Interior (Chicago), December* 10, 1885.

" Written in a lively and forcible style, and is one of the books which it is a pleasure to pick up when one wishes entertaining reading matter for a short time.—*Boston Times, U.S.A.*

www.ingramcontent.com/pod-product-compliance
Lightning Source LLC
Chambersburg PA
CBHW020811060726
47498CB00017B/1465